John Hovey Robinson

The Black Knight

Or, The wandering Bohemian

John Hovey Robinson

The Black Knight
Or, The wandering Bohemian

ISBN/EAN: 9783337194949

Printed in Europe, USA, Canada, Australia, Japan

Cover: Foto ©Andreas Hilbeck / pixelio.de

More available books at **www.hansebooks.com**

ROMANCES FOR THE MILLION

THE BLACK KNIGHT,
OR THE WANDERING BOHEMIAN

THE ABDUCTION OF DONNA TERESSA

GLASGOW & LONDON. CAMERON & FERGUSON

No I.

THE

BLACK KNIGHT;

OR,

THE WANDERING BOHEMIAN.

BY

Dr J. H. ROBINSON.

———————

LONDON:
THE GENERAL PUBLISHING COMPANY,
280, STRAND, W.C.

THE BLACK KNIGHT;

OR,

THE WANDERING BOHEMIAN.

———◆———

CHAPTER I.

A NOBLE knight, borne on a noble steed, journeyed amid the hills of Castile. He was clad
in mail from head to heel, and polished helm,
and cuirass of steel flashed in the sun. His visor
was down as when with lance in rest he rushed
to meet the infidel Moor. Upon the crest of his
helmet he wore the favour of his lady - love,
according to the usage of that period His
broad baldrick was studded with stones of
value, and a blade of costly fabric depended
therefrom, whose jewelled hilt displayed the
form of the holy cross A formidable battle-
axe swung at his saddle bow: woe to the knight
who should feel its weight. The horseman was
of a goodly size; his features could not be seen.
Proud and noble in his bearing, and fearless
withal, he bestrode a powerful white steed,
which carried him gallantly bedient to the
gauntletted hand that shook the rein. The
strength to endure and the lightning of speed
were in the beautiful limbs. He went forward
at an easy pace. A little in the rear of the

knight rode the squire. Like his master, he was
clad in mail, though of a texture less costly.
He was of lighter figure, and his years apparently fewer in number. His visor was up and
displayed features young and handsome. Gracefully he sat his steed, and light and easy was
his air. He bore the shield and lance, and
displayed the penon of his lord with beseeming
pride.

"Who comes hither, Garcia?" said the
knight, pointing to a horseman away in the
distance.

"Some seems he like a knight of Calatrava,"
was Garcia's reply.

"His sombre appearance would favour the
idea, good Garcia; and yet methinks he has not
a monkish bearing."

"True, sir knight, and yet as he approaches,
I see nought to hinder him from being a knight
of the order of Calatrava. And look you, my
master, he wears no favour of lady bright in
his towering crest."

"By my lady! he rides gallantly, whoever
he be. I would give a purse of gold to break a
lance with the stranger knight, be he gentle or
be he simple. He is encased in plate and mail
of a dark brown hue, and of tried steel stuff, I'll
warrant."

"Note you his haughty crest, Sir Haro?"
asked the squire.

"Yes, by my soul! it towers above all other
I have seen, as in defiance. I am not pleased
with the stranger's crest, Don Garcia. See you
the heraldry upon his shield?"

"Ay, Sir Haro. I see a knight in full

armour, with a dagger in his hand, and his foot upon the neck of his prostrate foe."

"I must measure swords with this proud knight, if kingly courtesy will allow."

The stranger approached.

"A fair day to you, sir knight," said Haro.

"And a fair day to you if your interests be fair—and a knight of such goodly seeming can have no *foul* intent," replied the stranger, gravely, yet with equal courtesy, and yet with an air that did not exactly please Sir Haro.

"Whence comest thou, sir knight? to what order dost thou belong? and what art thou called?" interrogated Sir Haro.

"I come from whence I list—I go wherever there are wrongs to redress or lovely women to protect. I am of the order of Calatrava. I am called the knight of the *Iron Crest*. My face is towards Burgos, in Old Castile."

"Now, by my faith, thou art wrong, proud knight of the Iron Crest. Thy face is towards Leon, and thy horse's tail towards Castile."

"Then thou shalt set me right, courteous sir. But whence comest *thou*, thy order and thy name?"

"I come from Leon. ɪ am a knight of the order of the Golden Spur. I journey towards Castile to tourney. I am called the Knight of the Steel Cross. I am under a vow to break five lances for the honour of lady love."

"And thou wilt do it right gallantly, I trow. I will joust with thee, sir knight of the Steel Cross, and verily, thou wilt do me honour thereby—for who is not honoured by an encounter with a true knight and a hidalgo?"

"I accept thy courtesy as gratefully as it is given, thou of the Iron Crest. I know not thy estate or thy name, whether thou art a hidalgo or what not; but if thou art not, thy birth belies thy seeming."

"My deeds shall prove to thee what I am, thou of the Steel Cross and the bold front."

Each knight received his shield and lance from the squire, and addressed himself to the encounter. They were now in an open space, not unfavourable to the trial of strength and skill. They wheeled their steeds and galloped away in opposite directions, with an ease and gracefulness that showed them familiar with the joust and tourney, and all deeds of prowess. The charger of the stranger knight was of noble breed, and prided himself, apparently, in bearing his noble burden. He was of ebon blackness, and like that of Sir Haro, powerful in frame, and unexceptionable in limb. When they had put a suitable distance between them, they turned their horses' heads, and with lance in rest rushed to the encounter. They met midway, and Sir Haro was nearly hurled from his horse by the shock. The Knight of the Iron Crest maintained his seat like a statue of stone. At the second course, the lance of Sir Haro was shivered upon the shield of the stranger knight, while his helmet was borne from his head by the skill of the latter.

"By St Jago!" cried Garcia, to the squire of him of the Iron Crest, "Your master hath done a noble feat: he hath struck the crest of Sir Haro's helmet with his lance, and driven it from his head. Never before have my eyes witnessed such a wonder. Well may he be called the Knight of the Iron Crest."

Saying this, he galloped to his master with another lance. At the third course both knights put forth their prowess in such a manner that horses and riders rolled in the dust.

The squires hastened to their respective masters, and assisted them to rise and mount. Neither was much hurt. They journeyed together towards Castile in seeming good faith, but the pride of Sir Haro was deeply wounded, despite his courteous bearing. He had prided himself highly on his knightly prowess, and deemed there was not a lance in Castile that could match him. It was true that he had not now been vanquished, but he had been matched ; and though he felt some admiration for the unknown knight, he was deeply mortified. There was, moreover, a deep and yet romantic mystery about the Knight of the Iron Crest that perplexed him not a little. Whatever thoughts he cherished, he studiously concealed them from the knight, and they beguiled the weariness of the way by conversing of knightly deeds—the wars of Ferdinand with the Moors, and the contemplated siege of Seville. When within a few leagues of Castile, the unknown took a courteous leave of Sir Haro, and pricked away over the plain in another direction. Leaving the latter for the present, we will follow the Knight of the Iron Crest.

The knight rode rapidly through an uneven and broken country, until the sun waned low in the heavens. As its last crimson beams were departing, he drew rein and dismounted in a deep valley, where his squire assisted him to lay aside that portion of his armour that might encumber him in walking. Stripped of his plated armour, he stood in a simple haubergeon and hood of mail.

"Tarry thou here, Don Rodrigo, and if I return not ere another sunset, seek me yon- der." And the knight pointed towards a tower- ing cliff of rocks in the dim distance.

"The duty of the true squire is to serve his lord, and at his master's side, and between him and peril. Suffer me to attend thee, like a loyal squire," answered Don Rodrigo.

"Not now, Rodrigo. My good sword shall find its place between me and peril. It never failed in the hour of need."

"But see, thou of the Iron Crest, the sha- dows of night have gathered, and the times are full of danger. These wilds are infested with hordes of banditti. Thou mayest meet them in an evil hour, and fall by an ignoble hand —thou mayest perish like a base born, and no hidalgo."

"I fear nought. Rodrigo. My strong arm is a match for the robber host."

The knight of Calatrava strode away toward the cliff of rocks in the distance. His path thereto lay through forest and dark pass, for he approached it not by the beaten path. He paused more than once to find his way through the tangled underwood and stinted shrubbery. As the shades of night fell deeper and deeper, these pauses were more frequent and protract- ed. At length the knight found himself com- pletely bewildered, and wandered on not

knowing whither. Chance or fortune at length
favoured him. He suddenly emerged from the
thick woods, and stood beneath the high walls
of a castle raised upon the very summit of a
cliff. It was doubtless the residence of scme
feudal lord. He clambered up the ascent with
much toil and difficulty, for he took not the
accustomed way, but approached it by the rear.
The castle was surrounded by a high wall. The
knight examined the right wing. At a window
far above gleamed a light. The discovery
seemed to give him pleasure. Leaning against
the wall, he sang in a voice rich and manly :—

" I come from the land of the infidel Moor,
My blood hath drunk deep of the Mussulman's
    gore;
The foes of the Christian have fallen in fight,
The Saracen flies from the steel-covered knight;
He quakes when he sees him with sharp lance
    in rest,
And shuns the bold knight of the dark Iron
    Crest.

" I've fought for fair lady—I've battled for thee,
But, maiden, thy thoughts have dwelt never on
    me ;
Thine eye never saw me, and never thine ear
In the past heard the tones thou art listening to
    hear;
Yet I've battled for thee with stout lance in rest,
I am known as the knight of the dark Iron Crest.

" I'm found in the tourney—I'm found in the
    field,
When there's danger to dare—a good sword to
    wield,

There'll be tilting to-morrow at gallant Castile,
And bold knights in harness, and lances in rest,
Look out for the knight of the dark Iron Crest."

But who heard the words of the doughty knight? Fell they upon the ear of lady bright? Awoke they gentle thoughts in the heart of blushing beauty? or died they away on the dark night and echoing walls? The daughter of Don Lopez de Guzman was no unwilling listener to the strain. Well might Donna Maria bend her beautiful head in breathless attention, for never was song more gallantly sung. She raised the window gently, and not a word was lost. The deep rich tones awoke a strange echo in her heart, and undefinable thoughts sprang up therein. Her pulses came faster when the song was ended. But why sighed Donna Maria, the peerless? and why wished she to list that lay again?

Ask him deeper versed in woman than I. How many questions arose to her lips warm from the heart—questions she could not an-swer! Who was the singer? He was a knight evidently—but was he gentle or was he simple? And then the heart thoughts of Donna Maria whispered that he was noble—a true hidalgo—a genuine son of chivalry. She gathered up the words of the song. She learned therefrom that she had never known the Knight of the Iron Crest; yet how strangely familiar his voice sometimes fell on her ear. Here was romance and mystery in keeping with the age of chivalry, but with all this there came a painful shadow from the past. She hesitated no longer; she

tore the rich scarf from her neck, and threw it
from the window. The next moment the breeze
had borne it to the eager hand of the knightly
stranger, and she regretted what she had done.
She saw him press it to his lips, bow almost to
the earth, and his noble figure disappeared
down the descent, and amid the trees. That
night Donna Maria dreamed of the knight of
Calatrava, and of a gallant youth who knelt at
her feet on a bright summer day, long, long
ago, when the birds sang and the sun shone.

CHAPTER II.

THE TOURNEY.

ON the following day, dames and damsels and
gallant knights, trooped to the listed plain. It
was a goodly array, and many grey-headed old
men who had done their devoir years ago, in the
tourney and in the battle-field, vowed by their
patron saint they had never seen the like in Old
Castile. There were cavaliers there whose steel
armour shone like the sun, and ladies that were
peerless in beauty, and barbed steeds whose
gay housings swept the ground. Trumpets
sounded, and many shields with their various
heraldry were displayed at the entrance of
tents prepared for the reception of knights.
Donna Maria was there, and the QUEEN OF
BEAUTY. It was hers to award the several
prizes to the victors. The galleries were filled
with the loveliest daughters of Spain, and
many a lady bright looked about for her chosen
cavalier—her favour upon his lance or helm,
or across his breast. Many ribbons fluttered at

lance-heads, placed there by fair fingers, and gay scarfs were worn over polished steel cuirass and gemmed baldrick. When the trumpet sounded, and the knights rode into the lists followed by their squires, the heart of Donna Maria beat with an unwonted pulse, and she looked with expectant eyes amid the press for her scarf, which should mark the Knight of the Iron Crest. The cavaliers met at headlong speed, and there was a clang of steel, and a shivering of lances. Riders were hurled from their saddles, and barbed horses rolled with their riders in dust.

But there was one knight there whose name and lineage were unknown; who performed such feats of skill as were never seen in Castile. He struck the helmet of a knight upon the crest with such force as sent it rolling away in the dust. It was the helm of Sir Haro. The unknown wore a crimson scarf over his broad baldrick—the favour of Donna Maria, and in him she knew the knight of Calatrava.

The course was right bravely run; and well each cavalier did his devoir. The beholders rent the air with their high acclaims. When the sports were broken off for the day, a diamond ring was awarded the stranger knight, and he received it at the hands of Donna Maria, queen of beauty.

Next came jousting, and Sir Haro entered the list on prancing steed, and challenged any knight for the love of fair lady to joust three courses with the spear, three strokes with the sword, three with a dagger, and three with battle-axe. There was a momentary pau

Sir Haro was a bold knight, and expectation was at its height. Not long were they kept in doubt. The trumpet sounded, and a herald proclaimed the Knight of the Iron Crest, who rode gracefully round the lists, greeted on every hand by the smiles and encouraging glances of dame and damsel. The first encounter ended as on another occasion, by the unhelming of Sir Haro and the breaking of the lances. The sword trial was most obstinate, as were the strokes with daggers, which were concluded without any obvious advantage to either. And now the gallant cavaliers grasped their formidable battle-axes, and gave terrible blows, which resounded upon their armour like those dealt upon an anvil by some sturdy son of Vulcan. In this, the Iron Crest displayed fearful skill and superiority. He wielded the mighty instrument as if it had been a reed ; it gleamed in bright circles over his head, and falling upon the helm of Sir Haro, felled him to the earth, and he was borne senseless from the lists.

Again the Knight of Calatrava was hailed with high acclaims, and kneeling at the feet of Donna Maria, received the reward of valour. After this the squires jousted, and the sports were closed for the day ; but not closed were the wounds Sir Haro had received. In the joust of the squires, the squire of the unknown—Don Rodrigo—distinguished himself in a striking manner, inasmuch as he overthrew all who opposed him, notwithstanding his extreme youth. As he knelt at the feet of beauty to receive the reward of gallantry, he was permitted to press the fair hand to his lips.　A proud feeling of triumph swelled his heart as he rode from the lists. Great deeds were in his thoughts, and the old nobles of Castile said, "We will yet hear from Don Rodrigo."

At an early hour in the morning the sports were renewed, and went forward with much good-will. At the close of the tourney, a Knight of Leon, of known prowess, entered the lists, and challenged any knight to joust with him to the utterance, with sharp lances, for the love of lady fair. Instantly a stranger cavalier sprang into the lists. A herald proclaimed him as the "Black Knight," whose lance was ever sharp, and whose sword was never rebutted. A simple crescent was upon his shield for emblazonry, and it was dinted in many places, showing much service. Judging from his appearance, he was young in years, and trained to martial deeds; but his visor being down the matter of his age was left in doubt. His armour was in striking contrast to all in the list; it was of ebon blackness. Never a knight entered the lists who demeaned himself better. Familiar was he with the rein and saddle, and the ladies of Castile said the "Black Knight" was a hidalgo born.

"He sits a horse like a king!" cried Ferdinand, in admiration. 'Were he a cousin I should fear for my crown. And see! the bright eyes of the dames and maidens of my court are upon him. God grant he may do his devoir as nobly as he sits a horse."

He waved his hand gracefully to the ladies, bowed low to the king, and dressed his lance to the rest. It was a joust to the utterance, and a prayer went up from many hearts that the

Black Knight might ride unhurt from the lists. Instead of putting his horse upon his metal, he galloped at an easy pace to meet his adversary. The beholders marvelled at his careless air. When within a few yards of his man, his steed bounded forward like the wind, and piercing shield and cuirass, his lance head was buried deep in the bosom of the Knight of Leon. The latter was borne away wounded to the death. Ladies sighed, for he of Leon was a brave man. The victor waved his bloody lance, shook the rein, and swept round the lists challenging any knight to the utterance. It was accepted, and another knight was taken out wounded.

"This must not be," cried the king, and closed the joust.

Again the Black Knight bowed to the lords and ladies all, and upon his fearless steed swept from the listed plain, bearing with him the ring awarded by the ladies, and presented by the queen of beauty. A murmur of admiration followed his departing steps. Long did the ladies of Castile remember him of the crescent. Minstrels of that day caught up the theme, wove it in the song of the Black Knight, who came like a meteor, and disappeared as he came.

SONG OF THE BLACK KNIGHT.

"Ye gallants of Castile—ye maidens so bright,
Have ye seen—have ye heard of the ebon black
knight.
Who came like the Simoom who went like the
wind !
There are many hearts breaking that knight
left behind.

"His armour was blacker than woman's dark
    eye,
His figure was knightly, his bearing was high;
His arm was a tried one, and sure was his
    blade,
When he rode to the lists, when he bat led for
    maid.

" He bowed to the nobles, he bowed to the king
He smiled on the ladies who formed the bright
    ring ;
With his stout lance in rest he dashed over the
    plain ;
His foeman shall ne'er mount his good steed
    again,

"That knight did his devoir most nobly and
    well ;
And fair ladies sighed for the gallants who
    fell;
But longer they sighed for the matchless black
    knight
Who blazed for a moment then vanished from
    sight."

But he was not the only one who won
laurels there.   The Iron Crest came in for an
equal share of honour, and it was a question
who had acquitted himself most gallantly ; but
Donna Maria decided in favour of him who won
her favour—a favour imprudently given.

That very night, while the thousands of
Castile were sleeping, the king was in confi-
dential converse with the Knight of the Iron
Crest. They spoke of a deep conspiracy, which
if successful, was to throw open the gates of

Leon and Castile and bring down the myriads
of the Moslem power upon the Christians.
The Crescent was to rise and the Cross to
sink. Among the suspected persons, the king
named Lopez de Guzman and Don Diego de
Haro. The knight started and turned pale
when Ferdinand named Lopez de Guzman.
His emotion did not escape the eye of his
royal master.

"By St Jago ! sir knight, I more than half
doubt thy good faith," cried the monarch, laying his hand upon his sword.

The bold knight turned his head from his
sovereign and passed his hand over his eyes.
The words of the king had grieved him. 'Twas
but an instant that his face was averted; he
turned again to the king, and throwing aside
his mail, offered his breast to the monarch.

"Now, by heavens! I have wronged thee,
my kinsman," he cried, and strained the knight
to his royal bosom.

"Thou hast wronged me, my liege, but like
a generous monarch, thou hast more than righted
me. One would almost wish to be wronged by
Ferdinand, so noble is his repentance, so generous his nature," replied the knight, with a sad
smile, pressing the hand of his master to his
lips.

"Thou art a true man, my kinsman, and
there is no boon thy sovereign will not grant
thee. Forgive if the cares of governing a tur-
bulent people makes him hasty and suspicious.
This being a king is not the height of human
happiness."

The king sighed and continued—

"But this conspiracy, which I have good reason to suppose is on foot, troubles me not a little. These rebellious spirits are the curses of kings. Assist me, good Alfonso, to sift this matter to the bottom. Keep an eye upon Sir Haro and De Guzman. Let them be marked men. I have read mischief in their eyes. Situated somewhere mid the dark hills of Spain, tradition says there is an old castle; it has the reputation of being infested by banditti. From what I have learned from a wandering Bohemian, this has been the resort of the conspirators. Penetrate the mountain fastnesses, and lay its secrets bare. When this is done, seek your sovereign."

"Did the Bohemian give thee no clue to this castle?"

"None, save that it was away to the north."

"Knowest thou where the Bohemian may be found, my liege?"

"Ask the king if he knows the way of the wind, or the path of the flying cloud. He is of the race that have no abiding place. Like birds of passage they are here to-day and away in another region to-morrow."

"Send forth a herald, my liege, and let the Bohemian be found."

"A happy thought; it shall be done, Alfonso, with a right good-will."

On the following morning a herald went forth and cried that the wandering Bohemian who recently had speech with the king should seek his presence without delay. On the second day the Bohemian made his appearance; he was covered with rags, and maintained a sullen

silence when in the presence of the king. Gold
was put into his hand, and he finally agreed,
induced by the promise of a large reward, to
conduct the knight to the mysterious castle.

CHAPTER III.

THE INSULT.—THE BLOW.

'TWAS night at Castile. There was hilarity and
music at the palace of the king. The knights
and nobles of the land were there, and happy
in the smiles of beauty. Among the revellers
were Lopez de Guzman, Diego de Haro, Alfonso
de Vivar, Don Rodrigo, son of the latter, Count
Lozano, and other distinguished names. Count
Lozano was a brave knight, of tried prowess,
but hasty and imperious. His loyalty had been
more than doubted by his sovereign, on the
occasion of several revolts which had disturbed
the tranquillity of the realm. Between him and
the aged Vivar, a very strong friendship had
never subsisted. The latter was now well
stricken in years, and the white frost of many
winters lay upon his head, and the deep traces
of time's finger were observable upon his visage.
He was frank and honest—true to his country—
true to his king. The wars of the Cross with
the Crescent were subjects of conversation.
Various opinions were advanced in relation to
the final success of the Christian arms. Lozano
was inflamed with wine.

" The Cross shall recede and the Crescent
shall advance. The Koran shall usurp the
Bible, the Prophets, the Christ," cried Lozano.

" Not so," said de Vivar, mildly. "Thou

art filled with with wine, Count Lozano. Th
Cross shall rise above the Crescent."

"Thou art in thy dotage, de Vivar.   Tho
shouldst leave such matters to younger an
clearer heads," retorted Lozano, insolently.

The old knight felt the insult. Bending fo
ward, and looking steadily into the face of Lo
ano, he replied :

"Unle s there be traitors among us, Lozan
the Crescent can never be exalted above th
Cross."

"Who spoke of traitors, old man ? Wh
mean y u ?" cried the count fiercely.

"I mean as I affirmed, rash count—th
Cross can only fall by treachery."

"Beware how thou dost tempt me, lest
forget thy age, dotard. I am no traitor."

"I said not that thou wert; and yet m
words stung thee sorely.   In turn, I bid the
beware, ount Lozano. Thou art too sensitiv
for a true man."

The Count sprang forward, and dealt the ol
man a vile blow.   Instantly a score of sword
leaped from their scabbards, and many voice
ried shame. All was confusion ; and then
would have been blood shed in that goodly com
pany, ha not the youthful Rodrigo sprang for
word and claimed the right to redress hi
father's wrong with his own hand.

The tumult was hushed. Vivar declared i
his pleasure that his youngest son, Rodrig
should retrieve his honour. But there was onl
one subject in connection therewith which wa
deeply embarrassing to the youthful Rodrig
The count had a daughter—Ximena—with who

charms he was enamoured. How could he meet the father of the maiden he loved in deadly combat! But the wrong of Vivar must be redressed, though the father of Ximena fall and the young dream of love be broken forever. That night was one of sleeplessness and distraction to Rodrigo. He dwelt upon the stern duty he was to perform on the morrow. He saw his aged parent writhing beneath an insult which nothing but blood could wash away. He saw the father of Ximena stretched lifeless and bleeding by his own hand, and heard the lamentations of the beautiful loved one. More than once he was on the point of throwing himself upon his own sword, and leaving the wrong to be redressed by an older brother. But no—his duty was plain, and he scorned to shrink therefrom. Should he prove the victor—which he doubted not—Ximena would turn with horror from the slayer of her father. He should hear no more the soft music of Ximena's tones—sun himself no more in the light of Ximena's eyes.

Long ere the bright morning dawned, Rodrigo stole from his chamber, and sought the mansion of Lozano. He wished to be near Ximena once again without feeling that he was abhorred—that there was no place for him in her young heart. He sat down beneath her window, and abandoned himself to melancholy reflections. In the silence of his own chamber he had woven his thoughts in song, and now in tones of sadness he sang them, while every note seemed to wake up an echo of sorrow in the deserted streets of Castile:—

"Ximena! Ximena!
    Thy love is near,
But the tones that thou hearest
    No more shalt thou hear;
The good steed that bears him
    Is saddled in stall—
By the hand of Rodrigo
    Lozano shall fall.

"Ximena! Ximena!
    'Tis night in Castile :
But 'tis day to the darkness
    Thy spirit shall feel
When, waking from slumber,
    Thou hearest with dread
Lozano is sleeping
    The sleep of the dead.

"Ximena! Ximena!
    Rest on till the dawn,
Nor ask where thy lover
    In sorrow hath gone;
The hope of his love-dream
    Forever is o'er;
What boots it he fall
    By the Infidel Moor?

"Ximena ! Ximena !
    I'll worship thee still,
Though destiny bear me
    Wherever it will ;
Though I fly to the mountain,
    Or fly to the plain,
And gaze on Ximena
    No, never again.

The good steed that bears me
Is saddled in stall—
By the hand of Rodrigo
Lozano shall fall."

Early in the morning there was a meeting to
the utterance, between Rodrigo and Lozano in
the presence of the king.

"Where is my foeman?" said Lozano, con-
temptuously, as he entered the lists.

"He is here Lozano," replied Rodrigo.

"Where, good Rodrigo? I see him not,"
retorted Lozano. "I see only a beardless boy.'

"Thou shalt feel him though thou seest him
not. Behold in the beardless boy the avenger of
Alfonso de Vivar."

They fought with battle axes, and the youthful Rodrigo demeaned himself so gallantly that
the count was slain. This feat of arms was
blazoned abroad, and became a matter of history
in the records of Spain. Without breathing
from the fight, Rodrigo put spurs to his horse,
and left the scene of his victory and his disappointment. How could he stand in the presence
of Ximena after slaying Lozano! Away, Rodrigo, away! love smiles no more for thee in
Castile!

Far away from the gates of Castile, Rodrigo
waited for the knight of Calatrava and the
wandering Bohemian guide. The latter was
attended by his spouse—a being gaunt and
bony, with a fierce black eye, a voluble tongue,
and hair coarse, like a horse's tail. Deeply
versed was she in the lore of her race. She
could read the life-lines upon the palm, tell the

destiny of dame and maiden, by power unknown.

"Draw the steel glove from thy hand, O thou
busno, and let me divine the lines upon thy
palm," said the wild being. Rodrigo held out
his hand. She examined the lines therein long
and attentively

"Raise thy visor, hidalgo. Thou wert born
in a happy hour. Kings shall envy thee—prin-
ces shall strive to emulate thy deeds—noble
knights shall follow in thy train, and bear thy
pennon with pride. When thou art the bulwark
of the sovereign's throne, oppress not the poor
Bohemian, O thou of the happy hour."

With a sign of respect she left him.

"Show no partiality, dark sorceress," said
the knight of Calatrava, with a smile, holding
out his hand to the gitana. She bent her dark
flashing eyes upon his broad palm.

"I would that thou wert my son, O thou of
the Iron Crest; then would the miserable Bohemian know a season of rest. In the future
there is power for thee, and away before thee.
When the good time coming has come, forget
not the wretched being who, once on a time,
read thee thy goodly fortune.

The noble features of the knight lighted up
with a strange fire. He dropped gold into her
hand, saying eagerly, almost sternly,

"Go on, woman, go on!"

"There is no more, Don Alfonso; bide thy
time. A helmet will not always bind thy
brows. When thou art the dispenser of life and
death, be merciful to my people. I have done:
question me no more—my lips are sealed. The

rack could not wring from me more this day"
and the strange wayward creature fell sullenly
in the rear   Don Alfonso pressed her in vain
to reveal more.

"Thinkest thou, hidalgo, that the poor
gitana has no thoughts of her own—no cares to
brood over?   Thinkest thou my race was made
only for pleasure, like a wretched beast of burden?   What seeks the high born knight of
the low-born despised Bohemian?"   And the
sorceress laughed in derision.   "When thou
shalt be what thou art not now, and the Bohemian woman shall seek thee with a boon to
crave, thou wilt say, 'Begone thou daughter of
darkness, begone?'"

"I swear to thee, wayward being, that in
the good time coming I will prove thy friend.
By this token I will know thee, and ask what
thou wilt.'

Don Alfonso placed a beautiful ring upon
one of the dark fingers of the sybil. This done,
he rode to the side of the squire, who had
hitherto maintained a moody silence.

"When the good time has come, I will see
thee," said the woman, as he left her.

"What thinkest thou of my fortune, thou
of the happy hour?" asked Alfonso.

"I believe nothing in the babblings of
yonder dark woman. This day's work proves
that I was not born in a happy hour. In good
sooth, I have heeded but little of thy converse.
I am not in a mood to listen to aught this day.
I wish no longer to live."

"Nay, gallant Rodrigo, why shouldst thou
despond? Thou hast proved thyself the boldest

youth in Castile, and many a lady bright wil
sing thy prowess—reward thee with her smiles.'

"Have I not this day slain the father o
Ximena the peerless? And yet thou dos
speak to me of the future, and the smiles o
lady fair. I will throw myself upon the lance
of the Moor, and die a glorious death. I wil
die in helmet and cuirass, with shield on m
arm, and brand in my hand."

"Lozano but suffers for his insolence. Lik
a true knight thou hast done thy devoir
Should Vivar languish beneath a blow unre
venged? Will Ximena despise the knight wh
avenged the wrongs of feeble old age? Not so
Rodrigo. Thou shalt kneel at her feet again-
she shall look on thee without abhorrence. Le
time do its work, and then shalt thou seek he
in knightly guise. This service we are on wil
I perceive, be one of adventure and danger. an
of a tendency to divert thy thoughts. Tho
wilt retun with new honours, and Ximena wil
not prove unkind. A living dog, runneth th
old adage, is better than a dead lion—a livin
husband shall atone for a dead father."

"I like not thy speech too well, my lord. I
thy servant a dog?"

"I crave your patience, Don Rodrigo—
meant not so. But see! who sits on yond
rock, as stirless as the rock itself?"

The squire raised his eyes. Some way i
advance a man was seated upon a rock
apparently unobservant of all.

"Seems he not like a palmer, sir knight
Wears he not a palmer's weed?"

"Thou art right I trow. As we draw neare

I see his pilgrim staff beside him, and the escalop-shell upon the centre of his crosslet. He has a rosary in his hand, and assiduously tells his beads. He is from the tomb of the Christ. He bears branches of the palm. His features are scorched with the suns of Araby and Ind. His sandals are worn with travel. He rises as we approach, and signs himself with the sign of the holy cross."

"Ho, good palmer! how fares it with thee? What tidings bringest thou from the shrine of our Lord?"

The palmer crossed himself.

"The pilgrim fares better than his deserts, sir knight, but the way is long, the sands are hot, and the suns are fierce and much oppress me. I return from the holy sepulchre weary and worn. There is but little news from the city of the Christ—the Infidel still desecrates the tomb of the blessed," replied the palmer, in solemn yet courteous voice.

"Whither goest thou now, good palmer, with escalop-shell and with pilgrim-staff, bearing branches from the holy city?"

"I am under vows. For deeds I may not name, I traversed the burning sands, but my vows are not yet redeemed. For a term of time must I sojourn in the mountains of Castile, Spain, subsisting only upon what providence shall throw in my way. Thither am I wending my way-worn steps, leaning upon my pilgrim-staff."

"Thither am I sojourning also, thou from the Saviour's shrine. Thy steps totter, and thy staff can scarce support thee. Mount thou behind the Bohemian, and rest thy fainting frame. Thy presence shall beguile the loneliness of the way."

"The palmer must trust to providence alone, courteous knight."

"And providence now offers thee a horse. See that thou slight not providence."

"There is wisdom in thy speech, thou of the dark crest. I will not refuse what providence throws in my way and urges upon me. Come hither thou swart son of Egypt, and I will mount behind thee."

With a sullen air the Bohemiam complied. The palmer vaulted up behind him, but was obliged to sit not in knightly fashion, on account of his long woollen garment, which, when standing, swept the ground.

"How is his gracious majesty, Ferdinand? Sits he firmly upon the throne, and governs he equitably and well?"

"Our royal master is well," replied the knight, "and sits firmly upon the throne. He governs with discretion and leniency."

"How fares his noble kinsman, Don Alfonso, of whose deeds I have heard from wandering minstrel, palmer, and knight."

The knight gave the pilgrim a searching look; but tone nor expression gave token that he had knowledge of the person he was addressing.

"Like his royal kinsman, he was in good health and spirits yester e'en. Knowest thou aught of him?" asked Don Alfonso, carefully.

"I know nought of him save by common

ame, which speaks him a matchless knight, and deeply in the confidence of his sovereign."

The knight smiled, and was not displeased.

" What say they of him good pilgrim ? "

" His feats of arms are extolled everywhere. His prowess is held in mortal dread by the Infidel Moor. I have heard it said that the king of Toledo, the great Ali Maimon, is the only heretic who wishes to meet him with shield on arm and lance in rest, on listed plain or the embattled field."

" I have heard much of Ali Maimon. He is a magnificent monarch, and Infidel as he is, I would give my best steed from stall to break a lance with him."

" Thou art generous to the Infidel, sir knight. Didst ever see him ? "

" I have seen Ali Maimon, good palmer, in mid battle, upon his peerless Arabian—in bright harness from head to heel—with battle-axe in hand, breaking Christian skulls, and cleaving Christian helms. Wherever arose the war-cry of Ali Maimon, the fight was hottest, and there was a terrible path wherever his crest was seen. And I have seen him with lance in rest, and panted to meet him, but the thousands of Spain closed in and shut him from view. The Cross is in danger when Ali takes the field. He is said to be noble and generous. Canst tell me aught of him ? "

" I know little of him. He is dreaded by the Christians, and is always engaged in war, as is known to thee. He is loved by his people, and not wanting in kingly courtesy. Knowest thou Sir Haro and Lopez de Guzman ? "

" I have met them oft."

" How stand they with the king? If I :
member rightly, their loyalty has been call
in question, in the past."

" I have but little knowledge of the knigl
thou namest. I have been absent from Cast
for a long time."

" Thinkest thou they are not suspected p
sons ? " And the palmer sent a searching lo
upon Don Alfonso.

" It is possible," replied the knight, in l
turn scrutinising the palmer.

" I thought as much."

The knight was silent. The palmer cros
himself.

" Don Alfonso has a sister? " resumed
palmer, interrogatively.

" He has, palmer."

" Report speaks her beautiful."

" The sister of Alfonso is fair."

" Has she suitors, courteous knight ? "

" Many, pilgrim of the staff."

" Who is the fortunate one, thou of the da
crest ? "

" Ask the maiden. I know not."

" It has been said that she loved one hosl
to our faith," continued the palmer.

" I have heard something of this nature,"
plied the knight of Calatrava, coldly, " but hi
given little heed thereto. The gossip of l
multitude is not always sooth."

" I have heard that her favour is worn by
unknown Moorish knight. Thinkest thou l
gallant Alfonso would consent to such
union ? "

"Never, palmer, never! The blood of the Christian cannot mingle with that of the infidel. There is a barrier between Donna Teressa and the Moorish knight that cannot be overstepped."

"Thou speakest earnestly, thou of Calatrava," said the pilgrim gravely.

The Iron Crest was silent and thoughtful. The conversation flagged. The knight pricked a little in advance. The Bohemian and palmer were alone; they were soon in close converse.

"How long wilt thou journey with us, O thou bearer of palms?" asked the Bohemian.

"I cannot tell thee, O thou son of Roma. Meet me at midnight to-morrow in the dark vale beneath the weird tree, away to the right of the castle yon knight is seeking. And harkee! mind well that thou dost not play me any of the cursed tricks of thy race. Look well to thyself."

The palmer gave gold to the Bohemian, and leaping from the horse, sat down by the way as before. The cavaliers moved on, and in the abrupt windings of the rugged way were hidden from view. The palmer was alone. His figure no longer looked bowed and weary. He stood proudly erect. His visage was no longer solemn, though grave and dignified. He drew a silver nail from his pocket, and blew a shrill blast. Before the echoes had died away, the sound of horses' hoofs were heard upon the flinty rocks in rapid approach. A squire appeared, leading a peerless Arab steed, barbed and housed. The palmer threw off his weeds—his long garment, cross and escalop-shell. Beneath his pilgrim dress was a coat of mail. Donning a helmet,

boots and spurs, he stood the black knight, as
he appeared in the listed plain. He shook his
lance, and vaulted into the saddle without the
aid of stirrup or rein. "Hi!" and the black
knight is off like the wind, over hill and dale,
through pass and fell, away towards Castile.
'Twas more than noon. At nightfall he was in
the environs thereof. A short distance from
him, in the outskirts of the city, a castellated
mansion reared its frowning walls.   When
night had fallen darker, leaving his Arabian
in charge of his squire, he directed his steps
towards the castle, bearing with him—strange
accompaniment for the sword—a minstrel
harp. Lofty was the structure he approached,
and darkened by the busy cycles of time. For
centuries had it been the dwelling of lord and
knight, and dame and damsel of royal lineage.
Kings had been born there.   Now it was
tenanted by women, and a few old knights and
aged vassals   The knight gazed long and
thoughtfully at the venerable pile—asked himself more than once if the Crescent would ever
take the place of the Cross that rose from its
highest tower, seen darkly in the dim moonlight.
    "The triumph would bring me no pulses of
joy should it bring scathe to Teressa the peerless," sighed the cavalier. "This fabric has
given birth to a line of kings, whose religion
it has been to scatter desolation and misery
throughout the land of Moslem. Would to
heaven the revelations of the Almighty had been
more explicit, and limited to no race of people
Then had been more goodness, and less dissen-

sions. But this is no time for such reflections.
I have come to woo and not to war. Like a
true knight, feuds shall be forgotten in the
smiles of lady-love. I will see if the hand
that can hold the spear can strike the harp,
and the voice that is loud in battle can im
provise."

The fingers that were wont to be gloved in
steel swept skilfully the strings of minstrel harp
Wild was the prelude ere the strain was sung—
eccentric and rhymeless the strain :

> " Rest, lady, rest !
> Far wanders the spirit of night—
> Its shadows lie dark on the hills.
> The night-bird sings—sadly the unseen winds
>   are sighing ;
> Dim is the waning moon, and dimly the stars
>   look down on lady's bower ;
>   Rest, lady, rest !

> " Dream not of the infidel Moor !
> He is false to thee—he stumbles in the walls of
>   Toledo.
> His blade is rusted in its sheath ;
> Ne'er strays his thoughts to Castile—ne'er
>   dreams he of thee.
> Recreant is the Crescent knight to the daughter
>   of the Cross ;
> He does battle for Moorish maid—for Infidel
>   ears tunes he the minstrel harp.
> Forgotten art thou ;
> Thy heart is sighing for the recreant knight .
>   Wake, lady, wake ! "

There was a pause in the strange measure. A

B

window was thrown up. In the pale moonlight
the fair features of Donna Teressa were dis-
cernible. She smiled and waved her hand. To
her the wild measure was no paradox. She se-
cretly approved the cautious manner in which
her lover had made known his proximity. She
trembled for his safety. Again the knight im-
provised, and his words seemed to contain a
mysterious warning :

"Danger lurks in thy path—there is sorrow for
    the daughter of the Cross.
Beware of a dark-browed knight!
The dove strays not when the hawk is abroad;
When the wolf prowls the lamb should be in
    fold.
Wander not at nightfall—there is safety in the
    castle of thy sires, and the evil time is
    near.
My hour has come—my good steed waits—I fly
    to the dark mountain :
        Rest, lady, rest ! "

The cavalier turned on his heel to depart,
when from the window he heard the sweet voice
of Donna Teressa :

" Return, O return, to thy people again ;
  Thy warriors are waiting for thee :
O fly, or they'll wait for their leader in vain,
  And thy people thou never shalt see.

"The knights of Castile are sworn foemen to
    thee,
  And guarded are passes and plain;
Thy life is in peril—in peril for me,
  O fly to thy people again."

The song ceased. A moment the lady bent forward in the attitude of listening.

"Away, bold knight!" she said in a low voice. "I hear the sound of approaching feet. As thou lovest me, attend to thy safety."

"Did I attend to my safety as I love thee, I should be safe indeed I adore thee. I swear it here upon my knees, that I never before bowed to woman."

"Then by that love I entreat thee to fly. Each instant of thy delay is fraught with danger, O thou of the Crescent."

"Fear not for the safety of the Moorish knight. He shall not suffer scathe. He quakes not at the shaking of a Christian lance. To him, fear is unknown, and danger is pastime; but for thy sake he would hoard his life. To him, it will be a priceless boon if valued by thee. I will away at thy word. Forget not thy warning. There is danger near thee. At eventide thou wilt be safe in the castle. In the hour of trouble the Black Knight will be near. Adieu, my life."

The Black Knight had bounded away.

"Ho! who art thou?" said a stern voice, and a steel-gloved hand was laid roughly upon his shoulder.

"Take this, thou insolent!" cried he of the Crescent, and dealt the intruder a blow with his gauntleted hand that would have brought a giant to the ground. As he fell the moonbeams darted across his face, and revealed the features of Sir Haro. "Lie there, like a dog, thou of the steel cross!"

As the knight strode on, he muttered the word "traitor!" between his teeth.

When Sir Haro recovered his consciousness, his head was aching and bleeding. The light baccinet or casque which he wore had not guarded him from the effects of such a buffet. His proud heart was bursting with rage. He smote his mailed breast—he ground his teeth in vexation.

Upon his bugle he wound a blast—a blast fierce and imperative. Scarce five minutes had elapsed before Garcia appeared with a led horse. Sir Haro took his good steed by the bridle.

"Fly, Garcia, fly like the wind! Arouse my retainers—lead them hither on swift horse. Away! away!"

Garcia turned, struck the spurs deep into his horse's sides, and darted away through the darkness like an arrow shot from the bow. In an instant the clatter of his courser's feet was not heard upon the rocky way. Ride, Garcia!"

Sir Haro waited impatiently. The tramp of horses was heard. A moment more, and a full score of cavaliers drew up beside him with a suddenness that brought their coursers' haunches to the ground.

"Thou hast sped well, Garcia," said the knight.

"Ho, ye knights and squires! ride for your lives, beat every bush, watch every pass, and scan the plain, and when you find a knight in dark harness, bring him to me, dead or alive. Ride, cavaliers, ride!"

There was a clank of steel, a striking of spurs and a thundering away. For a brief pace their course was marked by a stream of fire.

Sir Haro threw his bridle rein to his squire, and strode fiercely away to the castle. In poor mood was he to woo fair lady. He paused where the Black Knight had stood. Upon his bugle he blew a blast gentle as the summer wind. Fair fingers threw up a window.

"Thy lover is here, sweet lady!" said Sir Haro.

"He is imprudent—he will take cold in the night air," replied Donna Teressa, lightly.

The Knight of the Steel Cross bit his lips

"Nay, hear me, dear love, nor answer thou in mocking mood. Thou wilt drive a true heart to despair. Here upon my knees I worship thee. Never will I rise until thou shalt say me a kind word."

"Then wilt thou stay there for ever. After what has passed, why shouldst thou seek me thus, Sir Haro? Have I not told thee I love thee not? Think not I will change."

"It is said thou lovest an enemy of our faith."

"And if I love an enemy of our faith, what is that to thee?"

"It is much to thee."

"What meanest thou?" asked Teressa, eagerly.

"Ha! have I interested thee at length?" replied the knight, exultingly.

"If thou art done I will close the window," retorted the lady, carelessly.

"I can tell thee something of thy Moorish lover."

"Perhaps I see his mark upon thy face,"
laughed Teressa.

"Now by my soul, lady, this shall cost the
dear."

Sir Haro sprang to his feet in a rage, a
smote his gloved hand upon his mail.

"Nay, be not angry, sir knight—I mea
not to vex thee," said Teressa, soothing
"What canst thou tell me of my lover?"

"He is a prisoner. Long will it be ere
mount his courser or shake a lance again."

The lady Teressa uttered a cry of pain, a
grasped the window-casement for support.

"In heaven's name, tell me all!" she gaspe

"Not a word more."

"I entreat of thee by thy knighthood."

"When I sued to thee on bended knee for o
kind word, I sued in vain. Now is my hou
my ears are closed."

"Then begone. Thou art a craven, and i
true knight. Generous and bold is he who h
earned his spurs. Thou art neither."

"His fate, lady—"

"What of his fate? Speak."

"Well mayst thou ask."

"I will speak with thee no more," repli
the lady, disgusted.

"There is one condition, lady, on which
will tell thee all; but this is no fitting time.

"Name it, and be quick."

"Meet me to-morrow eve in the rear of t
castle, and I will withhold nothing from the

"I dare not," replied Teressa, in a tremulo
voice, remembering the warning of her lover.

"Then thou shalt hear nothing. Fair drea

to thee, lady fair." Sir Haro turned on his heel
as to depart.

"Stop one moment," cried Teressa. "Is there
no other condition?"

"None, lady, none; and if ere this hour to-
morrow night thou meet me not alone in the
rear of the castle, thy lover shall die."

"I will! I will!" shrieked Teressa, as with
difficulty she managed to cling to the window-
casement.

"Remember, if thou shouldst fail me!" said
Sir Haro, in a menacing voice.

"I will not fail thee—I mean it. At this
hour to-morrow I will meet thee alone in the
rear of the castle, but thou shalt promise upon
thy knightly honour that no scathe shall befall
me."

"I swear it. No harm shall come to thee.
To thy pleasant dreams, bright lady. Good-
night."

Teressa was alone. She had ample time to
reflect upon what she had done, and lament the
fate of her lover. More than once she was disposed to doubt the truth of what Sir Haro told
her. It might be simply a ruse to betray her
into his power. She knew he was wanting in
honour, but deemed he would not be guilty of
falsehood. By a falsehood he would forfeit his
spurs, for such was the law of chivalry. He
could not enter the lists who had been guilty
of falsehood. Would Sir Haro incur such a
risk?

To confirm what he had asserted, she now
recollected of hearing the tramp of horses' feet,
and the ringing of steel, soon after her Moorish

lover had left her. Sir Haro might have bee
lying in wait for his coming, and with his me
at arms made him a prisoner. And then sh
pictured him wounded and dying for her. I
any event he would have little hope from th
mercy of Sir Haro. The Moorish knight ha
been guilty of loving her, and that was crim
enough to warrant his destruction. Wha
would the Infidel have to hope for from th
hands of a disappointed and malignant rival
Again, the tale might be a sheer fabrication
and then the meeting would be attended with
extreme danger to her person. Thus wa
the mind of Teressa tossed with conflicting
thoughts. Like a true woman, she resolved t
brave all for her Infidel knight. Come dan
ger, come death, come captivity, the die wa
cast—she would meet the Knight of the Stee
Cross. Ere the dawn, the retainers returned
one by one, weary and unsuccessful.

Mounting his high-mettled steed, when he
turned from the donna, Sir Haro flew awa
through the dark night like the wild huntsma
or a demon rider.

CHAPTER IV.

THE STEEL CROSS, AND THE BOHEMIAN.

DEEP in the lonely recesses of the forest, awa
towards the Sierra Morena—made by tl
mighty mountain chain, was a valley profou
and dark. By most of those who had kno
ledge of its existence, it was deemed uncann
and was shunned on that account. But tho
who were better versed in the history of th

secluded spot entertained different and more reasonable views. Such doubted not that it was the resort of banditti. Indeed, the locality was favourable to such lawless purpose. Its basin-like depth was covered with trees, and accessible by only one path. The robber might despoil the wayfarer, and flying from the tents of civilization, find here an altar of safety. It was the day following the last scene. The sun looked down from mid heavens. Two persons were seen entering the valley. The one seemed a knight. His steed was jaded, and his sides were lashed with foam. It was with difficulty that he advanced. How great was the contrast between the two horsemen. The one was covered with polished armour, with barbed steel and gay housings, while the other was covered scantily with wretched rags begrimed with dirt. In the first we recognize Sir Haro, in the last the Bohemian guide. The latter seemed to have lost something of his sullenness and irascibility.

"Thy miserable people find a home here, then?" said the knight.

"It is their home as much as any place," replied the moody being. "Few of them are troubled with homes. The zeal of the Christian will not allow them a long abiding place."

"Thou art an intractable knave. Thy tongue is full of bitterness."

"It is not the fault of thy people that it is not cut out."

"Wag it most quietly, or it shall be no person's fault that it is not cut out."

"In that case I might keep thy secrets

better, perhaps," retorted the Bohemian
bitterly.

"Beware how thou dost beard me, thou son of
darkness. Thou knowest not my mood."

"I care not for thy mood."

"Thou wilt care, by St James! I will transfix thee with my lance, if thou art not more
civil."

"Thou dost not dare, O thou busno," replie
the Bohemian, calmly.

"Ha! art thou so presumptuous?" cried the
knight, raising his lance so as if to strike.

"Thou darest not strike,' said the Bohemian
without the least emotion.

"Why dare I not?" vociferated the knight
very angrily.

"Thou wouldst but thwart thyself. I an
necessary to thee. Thou canst not act without
me. I am identified with thy plans. I form
part in the woof of villany thou art weaving.
One word of mine will brand thee a—" The
Bohemian paused, and bending forward in his
saddle, and looking steadily at the knight, raised
his finger.

The arm of Sir Haro seemed palsied. The
lance dropped quietly to its place. He bit his
lips, and looked at the Bohemian with terrible
malignancy.

"Thou art right. Thou art necessary to me,
he replied, in a hoarse voice.

"Now thou art reasonable. In this matter
there should be an equality."

"Equality!" And the knight looked at the
miserable being at his side in sore amazement, as
discrediting all his senses.

"In all matters of villany, sir knight, there is a kind of equality—a sort of fellow-feeling. It is true there is a species of respect which the lesser villain accords to the greater, but this conflicts not with my theory. In some instances, a question might naturally be raised, who is the greater villain; but there would be many ways of deciding this. To illustrate: I, a villain, employ a villain to help me do a deed of villany. The villain whom I employed would henceforth be my equal, if so be he proved the villain I took him for. In this case the villain would be bound to me forever. I could do nothing without the villain's approval, and the villain could draw on my purse at any time, because I should be in the villain's power."

During this speech the features of Sir Haro were literally convulsed with rage, and the foam gathered upon his lips. To hear himself and fortunes identified with the Bohemian, was like living coals in his bosom. He, a belted knight, compared with the vile scum! Degradation indeed! But his hands were powerless. The villain said truly, he was in his power. And as Sir Haro rode on, he planred a death for the Bohemian.

They were now in a basin-like cavity. The Bohemian whistled loud and shrill. From the bosom of the earth, apparently, sprang up scores of ferocious-looking beings, who brandished long knives and swords, and yelled discordantly.

"Back, ye vultures!" cried Sir Haro, as they pressed and thronged him.

"Fear not, Sir Haro; they are our friends."

"Our friends!" muttered the knight.

"Away, my fellows, and make ready what ever is eatable among you. Sir Haro will dine with us—dine with us beneath the greenwood bough."

As the tumbling billows subside after th storm has passed, so was hushed the sea of tur bulent tongues.

In a moment the ruffians had passed quietly away. The Bohemian led on to the home of the lawless brood. It was a wild subterranear retreat, extending far back into the mountair chain. It had its wild rooms, and its winding ways—its mysteries and its crimes

"You see that I have some power, and tha this alliance will be likely to prove beneficial t both, courteous sir," said the Bohemian.

"What alliance, thou son of Roma?" asked the knight, reddening with passion.

"That subsisting between us," rejoined the fellow, calmly.

"How can I be benefited, knave?"

"Thou shalt protect my fellows when in diffi culty."

"And thus cheat the gallows. And what ad vantage will that be to me?" asked the knight, suppressing his rage.

"We, in turn, will do thy dirty work and keep thy secrets. Thus will mutual good accrue."

The knight, with all his cunning, was taken in the toils—the meshes of the net were about him. He had advanced too far to recede. In deed, to take a retrograde step was impossible, had he been in a mood to do so. But he felt no disposition to abandon any of his purposes much less that which had brought him to the robber cave. He had only to humour the whims of his villain. and trust to his own ingenuity to rid himself of him at some future time. Moreover, he might, as he said, do his dirty work.

"Those fellows will obey thee?" he asked.

"To the death."

"This service which I require of thee will need boldness and despatch."

"My fellows have both."

"Thou knowest the castle where I met thee, near the walls of Castile?"

"Well, sir knight."

"Knowest thou Donna Teressa?"

"I have seen her."

"Thou and four of thy knaves must be in the rear of the castle this day at the hour of midnight. The lady Teressa will meet ye there. Seize her, mount her on a swift horse, and bring her hither. And look thou, if thou harmest a hair of her head, I will make thee food for the raven. If thou dost speed well upon thy errand, thy reward shall be in red gold, and no stinted share. Have you any fleet horses and coats of mail?"

"We have steeds swifter than birds on the wing, and away yonder i. bright armour."

"Take thy best steeds and thy brightest armour, and do thou personate me; but harm not the lady on thy life. Go and choose thy fellows, and let them be thy boldest."

The Bohemian obeyed, and soon returned with four ruffians, fitted, apparently, for any deed of daring.

" They look bold and trusty, upon my soul,'
said the knight, while he distributed the con-
tents of his purse among them.

" Harkee, villains ! " said Sir Haro, sternly;
"if ye harm the lady, or play me false, I will
hunt ye to the death. and throw your carcasses
to feed the crows. When ye have brought her
hither, let her be attended as befits her seeming
till I return, and rich shall be your meed
Away, fellows, away !"

" Thou wilt partake of our cheer ?" said the
Bohemian.

" I cannot stay a moment longer for a king,
dom. Ere an hour I must be far away. Let my
horse be brought."

" He has tasted our provender, and his tired
limbs have been rubbed," said the Bohemian, as
the horse was led forth.

The knight sprang into the saddle, and dashed
away with fierce bounds along the narrow bridle
path. The Bohemian turned to one of his men,

"I entrust this business to thee. At the
hour the knight has named I have an appointment which I must fulfil, or I hazard my neck.
Do thou bring the lady hither, as yon rascally
knight instructed thee. Bring her here without
scathe. Speed thou on thy deviltry, and I on
mine. Let us help these Christians tear each
other."

A few leagues from the dark valley, Garcia
awaited his lord with a led horse of powerful size.

" Thou hast brought me a horse in good need,
Don Garcia," said the knight. " Meet me as I
told thee." Mounting on the led horse, he resumed his headlong career.

Speed! thou of the Steel Cross, over mountain and plain, across morass and meadow, river and stream, over hedge and stile, chasm and crag, through field and fell Stay not where the way is steep, pause not where the chasm is wide, or the stream deep, falter not where the barrier is high, 'or knights and warriors are waiting for thee, and thy faith is doubted.   Speed, lest they brand thee as a double traitor.

Ha! thou knowest thy need, and dash it bravely.   Right gallantly does thy courser bear thee, though his nostrils breathe foam, and his sides are streaming.   Another hour like the last and thou wilt win.

As he pricked on his attention was suddenly drawn to a wild skinny being who seemed to hover like a goblin over the very summit of a beetling crag, under which he was to pass. For a moment the superstition of the time took possession of the knight, and it may be that his own wicked heart lent wild strength to such a feeling. The wild figure waved a scarf in her hand, like that torn from a warrior's breast, where the hand of woman wound it ere the fray. Her long hair flew like dark streamers on the wind, and as she shook her bony hand, and called shrill, in the twilight seemed she a thing unearthly. The steed of Sir Haro snuffed the air, reared upon his hinder feet, and refused to move on. The knight crossed himself.

"Help, for the virgin's sake!" screamed the figure.

"In the fiend's name, what art thou?" shouted the Steel Cross.

"I am a woman in distress.   By thy knight-

hood come hither, for here is a dying knight t
shrive "

" Woman, my business is urgent, and th
way is long," replied Sir Haro.

" And urgent is the need of the dyin
cavalier, and longer the way he is going. Th
duty is first to the dying. Throw thy bridl
rein to the nearest bough, and haste."

Sir Haro complied. A few hasty strides too
him to the woman's side.

" Where dies the knight ?" asked Sir Haro.

" Yonder, beneath the Eildon tree. It goetl
hard with him, for he is strong and dieth no
easily."

Sir Haro hurried whither she had pointed. A
man in armour was stretched upon the ground.
Beside him lay his cloven helmet. There was a
ghastly wound upon his head. A half inch
deeper would have sped his spirit without a
struggle. The shadows of death were settling
upon his upturned face. Its cold sweat stood in
great beads upon his brow, or mingled with the
crimson dye from his cloven skull. His breath
came like convulsions. As the woman had said,
he was a brawny man, and it went hardly with
him.

" O, death is hard to him who dieth by violence, and in full strength," she said.

Sir Haro bent over the dying man, and
grasped his cold hand. He put his lips to his
ear.

" Thou art dealing with death, brother. A
knight is here. Hast thou aught to say ere
thou pass to the dark shore ?"

The sound reached his dying ear. He opened

his glassy eyes. For a moment memory struggled with the conqueror of all.

"It is the voice of Sir Haro," he said, with feeble voice. "Thou hast come in my hour of utmost need ; but thou canst not help me. I am battling to the utterance now with one stronger than thou, and there is no earthly armour that can save from the deadly thrust. I have entered the dread lists from whence no living warrior can ride in triumph."

In the dying man Sir Haro recognized one of his retainers.

"Who dealt thee this fearful wound?" he asked.

"The knight in black harness. I met him here, and you see his work. I never shall sit my good steed again—I never shall shake a lance."

There was a pause. The dying knight was terribly convulsed. He went on with an effort, with his filmy eyes fixed upon Sir Haro.

"Have I been a true man, Sir Haro?" he asked.

"Thou hast been a true man," replied Sir Haro, with a voice that showed some emotion.

"I have been faithful in thy service?" he asked.

"Thou hast been faithful in my service as man could be to his fellow-man," replied the knight, earnestly.

"Then I will be faithful in death. After this hour it will be beyond my power to serve thee. In this extremity my reason is not clouded by selfishness. Treasure up what I shall say, for God and this hour give me a far-seeing vision.

Thou art doing a foul deed. Thou art getting
such a stain upon thy soul as no water can wash
away. If thou go on, there is ruin to meet, and
a death to dare. Two paths are before thee
Choose which thou wilt, for I swear to thee as a
dying man, that after this hour the power of
choosing will not be thine. In the one path
there is honour and happiness—in the other is
treachery and a grave. Look where the moon is
newly risen. When it is one hour higher, thy
destiny will be fixed. Within this brief space
thou must decide whether thou wilt die a traitor
or a Christian. As one on the threshold of eter
nity, I charge thee ponder well. To thee I have
been too faithful, and as the reward of my
wickedness. I die as the fool dieth. I feel that
am going—what a pang was that—hold up the
cross—put it to my lips—God be good to thee
my master—forget not my warning where i
the cross! Christ's mercy on me—farewell—
remember, an hour will—will—"

The limbs of the dying man straightened ou
convulsively. and with him there was no mor
time—it had lengthened into eternity. To Si
Haro it was a strange scene. He had see
knights and nobles die on the embattled field
with the flush of victory on their grim visage
but never death like this. He stood aghast ove
the stiffening corpse. His warning words run
in his ear—he pressed his hand in mental dis
traction to his brow. An awe stole over him
He felt that the dying man had told him sooth
and this to him was the critical hour—the hou
that was to shape his whole future existence
From the face of the dead he turned to the moon

and with pale lip watched its upward course.
It was telling the moments of his precious *hour*.
What should be his decision? Should he abandon his projects? Should he heed what he had
heard? His steed neighed. He started from
his reverie, and was moving away, when he was
interrupted by the woman.

"Who art thou?" asked Sir Haro.

"It matters not," replied the woman, sobbing
aloud. "It matters not who I *am*, or what I
was."

Sir Haro looked at the woman more attentively. Middle age was stamped upon her features—features that might in other days have
been handsome; now they were deeply impressed
with care. During the interview between Sir
Haro and the retainer, she had held one of his
hands, and wept upon it bitterly. There was
something in the tones of her voice that jarred
strangely upon the strings of memory. The
knight put money into her hand and was going.

"Wilt thou leave the corpse alone?" asked
the female.

"No, thou wilt tarry by it, or it will take no
hurt to let it remain alone till I send my vassals
to take it hence."

"I cannot leave it, Sir Haro," sobbed the poor
creature kissing the cold hand she held.

"It is but dust, woman," said the Steel Cross.

"And so art thou but dust, but thy dust will
upon a time want Christian burial, though thou
die not like a Christian," retorted the woman,
bitterly.

"What was this dust to thee?" asked the
knight, touching the corpse with his foot.

"Nay, touch him not with thy foot, for he was of gentle birth as thou," shrieked the woman, "This dust was much to me—more than thou canst tell—and he died for thee."

"Thou knewest the young man?"

"I knew him well, Sir Haro. He came of gentle blood, though his noble father was an arrant villain. His mother was fond and frail, and when the wretched woman brought the fruit of her shame to the light. he spurned her away. When years had passed, the boy was taken back to his father."

"Who art thou?" again demanded the knight, in a husky voice.

"Thou hast forgotten! No wonder! I was young and blooming, then. Years of sorrow work sad changes with the features—especially of the erring. I *was* Mina—canst thou tell me what I *am !*"

"And the youth?" the knight's voice faltered.

"Was *thy son.*"

Sir Haro reeled as though he had received a crushing blow.

"My God!" he groaned.

He threw himself upon his knees beside the body, and gazed thereon with unutterable anguish. In the dead cold lineaments he recognized his own features. The knight sobbed aloud. With a prolonged cry of agony he sprang up, and snatched the almost lifeless hand of Mina—held it a moment in his—threw a heavy purse at her feet, and the next instant the clatter of a horse's feet was heard in headlong course.

For a time we will leave the *hour* and the *man.*

CHAPTER V.

THE OLD CASTLE.

IN the days of feudalism it was no uncommon thing to find the castle of a feudal lord in some wild, sequestered spot—in the deep glen, on the high rock, in the dense wood, far away from the peopled city At the date whereof I write, many such could be found ; but there was never one of more gloomy grandeur, and around which a profounder air of mystery and doubt was thrown, than the one we have now in our mind. It was many leagues from the walls of Castile, in the wildest and most unfrequented part of Spain. It had stood there in its loneliness many centuries, unknown, or known only as something uncanny Curiosity seldom tempted any person to approach its crumbling walls. Those who had never looked thereon doubted its very existence, or regarded the tales that were told of it as they did many other things of legendary lore and doubtful authenticity. At the time to which we allude, no person knew its lawful lord, or, indeed, whether it had any. Few travellers passed that way, and those who heard of it preferred, if benighted, to pass the night in the open air rather than seek its shelter. Its great wings were crumbling, and some of its towers were fallen. Chilling and uninviting was its exterior. Some said that strange sights and sounds had been heard there ; and there unearthly revels had been held The deep moat around it was choaked with weeds. On the night of the last scene, steel-clad men were seen entering its time-eaten portals. Upon the drawbridge. which shook beneath the tread of belted knights, stood two men at arms, leaning upon heavy battle-axes. To these the knights uttered a single word before they entered the castle.

There was one among them whose sword-hilt had not the form of the holy cross, but of the crescent. He wore mail without plate, and a light casque was upon his head. His figure and his carriage were noble. The suns of thirty summers might have shone upon his handsome face. His step was firm and assured, and fearless the glance of his eye. Occasionally an expression of scorn seemed to play upon his lips. He shrank, apparently, from anything like familiarity with those about him. The deference the knights appeared desirous of showing him was coldly yet politely received. The steps of the cavaliers awoke dismal echoes in the deserted halls they traversed.

"Here ye may expect Sir Haro soon," said a man-at-arms who had led the way.

"Where is Lopez de Guzman?" asked the knight in the haubergeon and casque.

"He comes," replied a retainer of Sir Haro.

The door swung on its rusty hinges, and Don Lopez entered. He bowed with distant dignity to the Knight of the Crescent and those assembled.

Sir Haro came not. The cabelleros grew impatient. He of the Crescent traversed the hall apart. His manner was thoughtful and abstracted. An hour passed. The cabelleros looked at each other for explanation. None seemed capable of giving it. Each spoke low with his friend. aside. But Don Lopez de Guzman betrayed the most uneasiness. He paced the hall with visible agitation.

"I suspect treachery, Nugnez de Lara," he said turning to a knight.

"He dare not act the double traitor, Don Lopez," replied Nugnez.

"He who dare betray his king and country, dare betray his friends," replied the first speaker.

"You speak with bitterness, Don Lopez. In judging Sir Haro, thou art deal ng hardly with thyself."

"I am," returned Guzman, sternly. "I was a fool to come hither, or to listen to the words of the traitor knave. I was ever loyal, noble Lara, till this night."

"What mean you, Don Lopez de Guzman?"

"What I have said, my lord—no more and no less."

The speaker laid his hand on his sword.

"Nay, Don Lopez, keep thy anger to thyself, for, by heaven, thou speakest my own thoughts. This night's work may brand us traitors."

Don Lopez started at the word "traitor," as though a serpent had stung him.

"I like not the word traitor," he exclaimed.

"And I like it not, Don Lopez."

"Then let us leave this place ere it can be justly given us. Should Sir Haro prove a double villain, there is no power on earth that can save us. He may be even now with the king. Let us ride, my lord, let us ride."

"Let our horses be brought," said Nugnez de Lara to his squire.

The Crescent Knight approached.

"Dost fear treachery, thou from Toledo?" asked Don Lopez.

"I fear nothing, sir knight," replied the Crescent calmly. "Come, tell me what means this delay? I came not hither to loiter."

"We know not why comes not Sir Haro. We doubt his good faith. We are about to attend to our own safety, and advise thee not to neglect thine. Our steeds are at the door. We shall tarry no longer for Sir Haro. If thou art wise, thou wilt mount and fly to Toledo."

"Nay, but this is not as I had expected. I came hither with the expectation that certain important matters were to be disclosed to me, and certain traitorous overtures were to be made on the part of Sir Haro—propositions which he would fain have us believe are greatly for our interest. You see how he has kept his faith."

"Something unexpected may have detained him. Ye can attend to your safety if you like. I shall tarry for the coming of Sir Haro. Will ye betray me?"

"Upon my knightly honour, I will not," said Guzman.

"Nor will I," added Nugnez de Lara, warmly. "I wish you a safe return to Toledo. I regret that we have been duped by a villain."

With a bow the knights left the hall. These were soon followed by the others. In a moment they were heard thundering away. The Knight of the Crescent was left alone in the castle. Knights, retainers, men at arms, all were gone.

"This bodes but little good," said the knight. "I may be betrayed by this knave, but as I reflect on it, I think he dare not. Let it be as it may, I fear him not. Let me collect my thoughts. Three hours from this I meet the Bohemian. However, it is but a short way, and I shall have ample time to examine the deserted castle. What adventures may I not expect to meet — what mysteries unravel? With this torch in my hand I will mount these rickety stairs."

The Knight of the Crescent ascended the stairs. and examined many suites of rooms, whose chill loneliness partook of the dreariness of the tomb. Who had frequented these apartments in days long gone? Where were they now? They had passed on to their rest, and left scarcely a vestige of what or who they were. He entered a long gallery, to whose crumbling walls pictures in antique frames were still hanging.

"These, perhaps," said the knight, thoughtfully, "were the inheritors of this decayed pile. Here is an old man with snow-white locks, and this woman might have been his spouse. And here is a young maiden, who might have been their daughter—and beautiful she was, by the prophet's beard! Here is a noble young man, half covered with dust, and a brother or lover of the girl, I dare say. Ha! I thought I heard a step ; but no, it cannot be. I am alone. I will go up still higher. This might have been the bed-chamber of the lord of the castle. 'Tis cold enough, now. Here is a broken cross. What strange people are these Christians, to prize so highly a bit of wood! Hist! By the soul of Mahomet, I heard a footfall!"

The Knight of the Crescent paused and listened.

"My fancy must be playing tricks with me. I heard but the echo of my own tread. I will go on again. This might have been my lady's private chamber. Here is a dusty image of the virgin. Why do these Christians worship images? I pass on. I will look into this closet. Perhaps I—"

The Moorish knight was not permitted to finish the sentence. The light was dashed from his hand, and he was felled to the floor by a violent blow upon his head. When he recovered his consciousness, he was still lying upon the floor. His head ached violently. He was in total darkness, and scarcely knew what had happened. He arose to his feet, and stood for a moment to collect himself. He drew his sword, and with its sharp point he felt about for the door. While thus groping in the darkness, the wall seemed suddenly to open, and he felt a damp current of air upon his face. His sword point had touched a secret spring. The knight hesitated. Should he go forward, or should he recede? A sound below caused him to decide upon the former. He entered the secret passage and drew the sliding panel. He had scarcely done so, when he heard steps upon the stairs, and the ringing of armour. He heard armed men searching rooms beneath him. He heard them again ascend the stairs, and approach the apart-

ment he had just left. They were no doubt
looking for him, and were persons sent by the
Christian king to apprehend him. A sense of
his imminent peril came upon him. A cold
sweat gathered upon his forehead. The extreme rashness of the enterprise whereon he
had come, had never appeared so vividly as
now. What had he not hazarded by leaving Toledo? Not only his exalted position but his
life. The motive that had brought him into an
enemy's country might also bear various con-
structions. He had come to treat with a traitor
—a man whom in his heart he had despised
But this was not all. He had come hither also
to woo—to woo one hostile to his faith. The
man with whom he had come to treat for the
betrayal of his king, he had recently discovered, was his rival. He had met him but
a few hours before—had dealt him a blow.
The traitor might have recognised in his rival
the Infidel Moor. Prompted by revenge, of
what act might not Sir Haro be guilty?
Would he hesitate in betraying him into the
hands of his natural enemies, the Christians?
Certainly not. This might possibly have been
his purpose from the beginning. Such were
some of the thoughts of the knight, as he lay
in his place of concealment, and heard men in
armour crowd into the apartment he had just
left.

"This is the apartment," said one of the men
" And here is the closet where I was concealed.
I rushed forward, extinguished his light, and
struck him with my gauntleted hand, and, by
St Jago, I thought he never would rise again!

He is concealed somewhere hereabouts. He cannot escape "

Several times they passed his hiding place,
and even touched the secret panel At length, to
the great relief of the knight, they left the apartment, and proceeded upwards towards the central
tower.

Thankful for his escape from danger, although
he scarcely knew of what nature, he began to go
forward with extreme cautiousness for fear of a
fall, and on account of the pitchy darkness.

The passage was very narrow, and wound
gradually downwards towards the base of the
castle. Sometimes his passage was partially ob-
structed by the decaying rubbish that had fallen
and choked the way.   It had been long, apparently, since human feet had followed its secret
windings.   It had been used in days far back in
the past, for purposes that now could only be
guessed at.   How much mystery, adventure,
crime, perhaps, was linked with the history of
that secret way ! Fair maiden might have stolen
softly from thence to meet her lover by moonlight; bold knight might have unwound its windings to meet his lady-love—midnight assassin to
do a deed of darkness.

But this was no time for idle speculations.
The knight must by some means leave the castle
Some considerable time had elapsed since he
commenced the descent.   He believed himsel!
near the base of the castle, when the rotten
structure gave way beneath him and he was
conscious of falling. Luckily the distance was
not great, and he sustained but little injury
Somewhat stunned and bewildered by the fall

the knight regained his feet. There was something between him and the earth, and he was sure that he was at the base of the castle. He felt about him. The way was still narrow. A damp current of air came rushing to meet him; he went forward in the direction from whence it issued, feeling before him with his sword. Its edge came in contact with something hard like steel or plate. Instantly a man in armour leaped to his feet, and in the deep darkness there was the crossing of swords. Furious, though brief, was the contest that followed. The angry clash of their blades struck fire, and their edges were blunted upon each other's armour. The assailant was soon disarmed.

"Now yield thee, whoever thou art, or I will cleave thee from helm to cuirass!" cried the knight.

"I yield," said the unseen, doggedly.

"'Tis well. Canst thou lead me to the open air?"

"I can, if so disposed," replied the voice, moodily.

"Then do so, and it shall fare better with thee," said the knight.

"I fear thee not," retorted the unseen, roughly.

The knight heard him feeling for his weapon with his foot.

"Lead me hence," cried the knight, in a voice of thunder, "or I swear by the Koran thou shalt surely die!"

"Come on, then," growled the unseen, and strolled sullenly along the passage. The knight followed, with his sword unsheathed.

"Who art thou ?" he asked.

"No matter," was the morose reply.

"Now, by the prophet, thou art not cour
teous!"

"Neither art thou, Infidel," retorted the us
seen, in the same unconciliating tone.

"Why shouldst thou set upon me in the pas
sage unprovoked ?"

"Why shouldst thou be in the passage, the
unsanctified and unbelieving ?"

"Because it pleased me to be there, thou mo
uncivil."

"Then let it please thee to find thy w:
out."

"Thou art no philosopher—thou dost n
bear defeat with manliness."

"I care nothing about philosophy—I har
other matters to think of."

"That could not prevent thee from keeping
civil tongue in thy head."

"I have done thy bidding. We are in th
open air," said the strange being.

The knight had now an opportunity to sa
his unknown guide. He appeared, as he stor
there moodily in the moonlight, a man of lar
proportions, and possessed of much bru
strength. He was encased in rusty armou
which had seen much service. He threw
his visor, and the features that were left n
covered were coarse and savage. Both neth
and upper lip were covered with dark gri
beard.

"What is thy calling?" asked the knight.

"I have no calling."

"How livest thou ?"

" I live by dale and down."

" A hunter ?"

" Thou sayest truly. I hunt men. Ha, ha ! Fine sport it is. Didst ever hunt men, Infidel ?"

" I suspected thy calling, thou most savage. Thou art a bandit. This castle affords thee and thy fellows a shelter. I'll wager my best steed in stall that I have met one of thy fellows within the hour."

" Thou wert never nearer the truth. May perdition seize thee for thy intrusion. Hadst thou fallen in with my fellows, thou hadst been food for crows ere this."

" Thou hast fallen into my hands. What then shall be thy fate ?" replied the knight.

" I care but little. Do thy worst," was the sullen and almost fierce rejoinder.

" How many villains hast thou in thy service, thou of the moody brow ?"

" Twenty."

" Are they bold and trusty ?"

" They are as daring fellows as ever drew blood." replied the bandit, with an air of triumph.

" If I harm thee not and give thee thy liberty, wilt thou serve me in the hour of need ?"

" I will by my soul !" cried the freebooter, with a warmth he had never before manifested.

" On this condition thou art free to go where thou wilt. Here is gold for thee."

The knight put yellow pieces into the bandit's hand. For a moment the bandit gazed on the generous knight in doubt. Then he drew

a ring of value from his hand and placed it
upon one of the fingers of the vanquisher,
giving him at the same time a small silver call,
saying :

"When thou wouldst have aid in thy hour of
need, blow this call and show this ring. If thou
art within these wilds, the bandit and his
knaves will stand between the Moorish knight
and death."

The bandit waved his hand, moved slowly
away, and his herculean figure was soon lost to
view.

Not far from the castle was the weird tree,
where the Bohemian was to meet the knight.
Thither the latter now directed his footsteps.
The night was deep on wild and wood. The
moon was high in the heavens. Its pale beams
with difficulty struggled down through the
trees and lighted the warrior on his dubious
way. The ground before him was rugged and
lonely. Seldom was it traversed by night, save
by freebooter, or wild beast in quest of prey.
Well might the traveller expect at every un-
certain step to be greeted by one or the other.
The Moor was soon on the spot. The Bohemian was not there. The knight seated himself
beneath the tree. He judged it was near the
time appointed for the meeting. Some minutes
elapsed, and still he came not. The knight
grew impatient—arose to his feet and walked
forward to divert his thoughts. A sound came
to his ear, borne upon the low night wind. He
laid his hand upon his sword, and hastened on
in the direction from whence it proceeded. As
he hurried forward the sounds grew more dis-

sect. The cause was soon apparent—two persons engaged in fierce combat. The knight paused and watched the contest. In a moment a third person made his appearance, and there were two engaged with one.

" Cowards !" cried the knight, as he sprang forward to the aid of him who seemed to need it. " Is not one to one enough ? Have at you."

The fellows were taken by surprise, and fled. The knight turned to the person he had assisted. It was the Bohemian.

" Ha, is it thou ?"

" It is the wandering Bohemian—the hated of all races," was the cold reply. " He has come according to thy bidding."

" And it has well nigh proved fatal to thee."

" Well, what matters that ? Who would have wept for the accursed wanderer, save a wretched woman."

The knight gazed with pity upon the Bohemian.

" Thou hast been faithful to me—henceforth look upon me as thy friend," he said kindly.

" What wouldst thou have of me ?" he asked, abruptly, without otherwise heeding the gentleness of the Infidel knight. " I am here at thy bidding."

" Strange being !" muttered the Moor. "Thou dost want no friends, then ?"

" None—none. This is my friend, and you see I tread upon it."

The Bohemian struck his foot violently upon the earth.

" Thou sayest well. The earth is the friend

C

of all.   It sustains us while living, and affor
us a grave when dead.   Dear and deep is i
rest.   Where didst thou leave the knight
Calatrava and his bold squire ?" he asked, aft
a pause.

"Far away, many a weary league from th
in the Uncanny Vale, where dwell an uncan
people   There they watch for Sir Haro and h
treasonable friends   They will watch long a
they find them."

"Knowest thou aught of this traitor, S
Haro ?"

" I know that this night he hath much bu
ness upon his hands."

"What meanest thou ?"

" He has king to betray, and maid to wo
and a child to earth."

"Explain and be quick."

" Ere this hour, she thou lovest is sweepi
like the wind over the wild moor, borne
brawny arms."

'By the Koran, has Sir Haro dared— ?"

" Yes, he has dared—thy nest is robbed—t
pretty bird is caught."

"This very night thou sayest."

"This very hour."

"Tell me where—whither she is being c
ried, and I will fly to her rescue.   Speak ma
shouted the knight.

"Be calm," said the Bohemian, quietly.

"Speak to me again of calmness, and I w
transfix thee," retorted the knight.

"Be calm," was the cold impassive respon
while not a muscle of the Bohemian's face t
of emotion.

The Moor drew his sword half from its sheath, paused an instant, sheathed it, and said, quietly, "Take thine own way."

"She thou lovest is in the power of my ruffians. At this moment they are bearing her to our wild retreat."

"Thou didst lend thyself to this transaction then?"

"I did. Am I not in the service of Sir Haro?" he replied, with provoking coolness.

"Art thou not in my service, thou knave?"

"Is it not doing thee a service to tell thee where thy rival hath borne thy lady love?"

"Why shouldst thou help him?"

"That I might help thee and be cursed for my pains."

"Ha, I see it all. Thou hast done well. I have been too hard with thee. Much gold shall be thy meed."

The Bohemian heard with a cold sneer upon his lips.

"Thou wilt take me to her,?" said the knight.

"Ay, and be repaid with menaces!"

"No, thou and thine shall dwell in safety in the land of the Moor—within the walls of Toledo, if thou wilt. I swear it," rejoined the Crescent, with deep earnestness.

"To-morrow I will show thee the way."

Here the Bohemian explained all that had transpired within the last twenty-four hours.

"Thou didst say he had child to earth," said the Moor.

"And I spoke sooth. As I came hither upon my good steed, I heard the sharp cry of woman. I went thither. A woman wept over a dead youth. The youth had fallen by the hand of the Black Knight. It was the son of the traitor, and the woe-wild female was its dam. The young man died in his father's arms, and the latter, with a heart full of agony, mounted his courser and dashed furiously away."

The Moor grew thoughtful.

"I shall pass the remainder of the night at the castle. Thou canst pass it where thou wilt. Meet me here when the sun is up," he said.

"Is there not danger at the castle? "

"None for me, Bohemian, none for me."

The Moor returned to the castle and strode boldly in. At the gate stood a horse covered with foam, and panting as over-driven. The knight passed on and entered the hall. A man was seated there with his face buried in his broad palms. He seemed to be suffering deeply.

"The hour—the hour of destiny has gone for ever. My fate is fixed. Henceforth must I be the villain I have ever been. The hour of my moral salvation is dead. My course is on. I will study to be successful, even in my wickedness. Away with weak regrets, with unmanly repentance. One tear for my poor boy, one sigh for Mina, and I am a man again."

The Moor struck upon his armour with his steel glove. Sir Haro started to his feet.

"Ha, it is thou from Toledo!" cried the latter, in surprise.

"It is. Why lingered he from Castile?"

"Unexpected business detained me, but I have ridden hard to redeem my honour."

"Honour!" repeated the Moor, with emphasis.

The echoes of the crumbling castle seemed to catch up the word and repeat it a thousand times more than wont. Sir Haro bit his lips and reddened to the eyes.

"Thy steed gives evidence of hard riding," added the Moor. "Thy friends have been here and gone."

"In what mood went they, thou of the Crescent?"

"In doubtful mood, as fearing treachery."

Sir Haro strode about the hall much agitated.

"Will they betray us, thinkest thou?"

"They said not, upon knightly oath, or rather that they would not betray me."

"I fear them."

"I do not. What wouldst thou propose? Let us to business at once."

"The delivery of Castile into the hands of the Infidel king, Ali Maimon," was the reply.

"Name thy conditions—the price of thy treachery."

Again Sir Haro reddened to the brows, and made a motion towards his sword.

"Knowest thou the Black Knight," he asked, looking fixedly at the Moor.

"I know him well," replied the Moor.

"Dost thou regard him?" again questioned Sir Haro, still bending his dark grey eyes upon him.

"He loves the same woman that I do," replied the Moor.

The stern rigidness of Sir Haro's feature relaxed.

"Then I will be sworn thou lovest him not," he said, with a grim smile.

"Canst thou blame me?   Yet I said not that I loved him not."

"Yet thou didst say what pleases me bette —that he is thy rival, which means thou dos not like him."

The Moor smiled and asked:

"What of him?"

"Give him into my power, with a thousand pieces of gold, and the Crescent shall be raise at Castile."

"Will this satisfy thee?"

"I ask no more."

"It shall be done.   What wilt thou do with the Black Knight when in thy hands?"

"That will matter not to thee," replied th Steel Cross, sternly.

"Thou wilt rid the earth of him, no doubt thou follower of the Cross?"

"I said not what I would do."

"How wilt thou deliver to me the keys of Castile?"

"I will tell thee."

Here Sir Haro entered into the details of hi scheme.   It appeared satisfactory to the Moor

"I will consult with Ali Maimon," said th latter, "and meet thee here at the expiration o ten days.   And now show me some place to pas the remainder of the night, for my eyes ar heavy."

"Here wilt thou find but homely fare, bu the best is at thy service.   Step lightly upo these rotten boards. It is seldom they are pressed by knightly feet. Mount after me. Here is a lone and comfortless room, but the best I can offer." And he led the way to the apartment where the Moor had been so rudely handled.

The Moor bowed his helmed head to the dust —he invoked the prophet—he cast himself upon the floor in harness, and slept a soldier's sleep.

CHAPTER VI.

THE KNIGHT OF CALATRAVA AND HIS SQUIRE CONTINUE THEIR JOURNEY.

ON journeyed the knight of the Iron Crest, and he of the happy hour. The Bohemian guide pricked on and put himself before them.

"Where is the palmer?" asked Don Alfonso.

"The man in the woollen gown leaped from the croups, and I left him by the wayside mumbling prayers."

"I thought he would have journeyed on with us. I would hold further converse with him. Haste back, Gonsalez, and pray him to keep us company. Let thy speech be fair to the bearer of palms."

The Bohemian turned his horse's head, and rode back, but returned as he came.

"Thou sped not well on thy errand, Gonsalez," said the knight.

"The man of the staff and shell has gone his way," replied the guide.

Don Alfonso mused.

"Observed thou aught singular in the appearance of the pilgrim?" he asked of Rodrigo.

"I noticed nothing in him unbecoming palmer, save strength. He is stronger than wont for one who has traversed the burning sands."

The knight made no reply, and thoughtfully they pursued their journey.

The way was rough and hilly—the same Alfonso had travelled a few days previously, on his way to the lists.

At nightfall, Rodrigo and the Bohemian guide took lodgings at an inn; but Alfonso having refreshed himself, rode towards the castle of Lopez de Guzman. Leaving his horse as on another occasion, he clambered up the cliff 'Twas early night, and lights were gleaming from the castle.

"It will be long ere these fires are extinguished, and I must have speech with the Lady Maria, ere that," mused the knight.

At that moment the sound of minstrel harp came to his ear, borne on the winds of night.

"Ha, a thought strikes me. My hands have some cunning with the harp; and by my lady the minstrel comes this way—the heavy portals open, and close upon him Come hither, thou harper, for a knight hath word for thy ear, and gold for thy palm."

"What wouldst thou, noble knight?" asked the minstrel.

"Change thou thy minstrel garb and harp for the warrior's sword."

"Most uncourteous were I, most courtly knight, to refuse thy request so fairly urged.

When there is lady to woo, and love to win, the minstrel garb becometh knight."

"Right gallantly spoken, thou minstrel man. Thy tongue is acquaint with courtly phrase, May thy noble art never die. Lend thy hand to rid me of this case of steel. Now for thy garments, harper. I change—give me thy harp which thou hast tuned for lady's ear. Now I am in sooth a son of song. How look I?"

"Like harper good and true, and comely to gaze upon. Let's hear the prelude to thy strain. By St James, well thou strikest the strings. One would swear thou wert harper born."

"And two would swear that thou wert knightly born. Thou hast a warrior air—and stand like prince in armour. One would deem thou hadst worn knightly guise before. Ha, thou layest thy hand on thy sword as though thou wert familiar therewith. It were not strange that I should lay knighthood on thy shoulder yet. Wait my return, gallant minstrel. And now for the castle, and song for lady love."

A few notes upon his harp, and the massy portals swung again upon their hinges, for never among the knights and nobles sought minstrel shelter in vain.

"What would the minstrel?" asked the porter.

"Shelter for the night, and if it please him he would fain tune a humble lay for the ear of lord and lady."

The minstrel was ushered in, and refreshments were placed before him.

"Refresh thyself," said the porter, "for the

way is long which thou hast come. Here
wine whose age is equal to thine. Drink, min
strel, and the spirit of song will be strong upo
thee, and the strings of thy tongue, if not
thy harp, shall be unloosed. In this eloquen
beverage will I pledge thee, thou man of song
Mayest thou never get worse, and thy hand
grow never less cunning, or thy voice les
musical."

The porter grew loquacious.

"Whence comest thou?" he questioned.

"I am from Castile, and as thou sayest, th
way is weary."

"Thou wert there at the tourney?"

"Ay, I was there in good sooth."

"Now by the saints, thou must tell me of
this same tourney, whereof tales are in every
body's mouth It is said that gallant thing
were done there—that a certain knight, know
as the Knight of the Iron Crest, unhelmed Si
Haro twice by striking his crest, after which
he fought him to the utterance."

"How fared Sir Haro when they fought t
the utterance?" asked Alfonso, with a smile.

"Badly enough, I trow. With a dreadfu
blow of his battle-axe, he clove Sir Haro from
chin to chine, and he was carried from the list
in two pieces."

"Wonderful!" replied Don Alfonso
smiling.

"You may well say it," rejoined the porter

"What else affirm they of this fearfu
knight?" asked the minstrel.

"Ah, I dare not tell," he answered, glancin
cautiously about him.

"Another draught of this juice will make thee fearless. Here's hale old age to thee, thou courteous porter. Now what more of the famous knight?"

"They say that my lady loves him, and that once on a night he sang beneath her window."

"And believest thou this?"

"Every word of it."

"Why thinkest thou she loves the knight?"

"For reasons good. Donna Maria changes colour when I speak of the Iron Crest, and though she chides me, and says, 'What care I for the knight?' yet she lingers to hear me speak in his praise, and turneth oft to hear more."

"Whence cometh the knight of whose prowess you speak, and what is his name?"

"It is said that he came recently from the holy city, and the sepulchre of our Lord. At the tourney he raised not his visor, and no one recognised him. The knight is unknown, although it is whispered that he is known to the king."

"Had the knight sojourned long in the holy land, good porter?"

"I know not. I hoped thou mightst tell me."

"I have heard of the knight, but know little of him. He is from the Saviour's sepulchre, yet I hardly wist how long he has tarried there. He is noble I ween, and no craven. Hath Donna Maria suitors?"

"At present I believe she hath but one."

"And who is he?" asked the minstrel, with earnestness.

"The noble Nugnez de Lara."

"By St James, sayest thou so?" cried the minstrel.

"Ay, but why should it move thee? Thou carest not who the donna weds?"

"Thou sayest truly, I care not," replied Alfonso, recollecting himself. "Has the knight had speech with her lately?"

"It would be strange if he had not, for he hath seen her this day."

Don Alfonso grew thoughtful and silent.

"I have humble lay for thy lady's ear," he said at length.

"I will see if my lady will hear thee," and the porter went on his errand. He soon returned. "Thou art favoured, minstrel, for thou shalt tune thy harp to the ear of Donna Maria, the fairest lady of Spain. Follow me. Skilful be thy hand—sweet thy voice. Here is my lady."

The minstrel bowed low to Donna Maria. She smiled, and bade him be seated, in a gracious voice.

"My menial hath said thou hast lay for my ear."

"He said truly, fair lady. The wandering harper hath rude song, and rude measure for thee."

"Thanks, minstrel, thanks! With pleasure will I list thy lay. Whence comest thou?"

"I am now from Castile, and recently from the Saviour's shrine."

"Ah, sayest thou so—knowest thou—" The lady spoke eagerly, but checked herself, while a blush of crimson hue suffused her face and neck.

"Of whom wouldst thou ask, lady fair?"

"It matters not.   I will list thy song," she replied with evident embarrassment.

With a short prelude he sang:

"A pilgrim came from holy land,
    No palmer's weeds he wore,
Nor scallop-shell—and in his hand
    No pilgrim staff he bore.

"He came with helm upon his head,
    With cuirass on his breast;
With his good sword upon his thigh,
    And his stout lance in rest.

"'Twas thus he sought the listed plain,
    To joust for lady dear,
And those who fell rose not again,
    To wield the sword and spear.

"Thou shouldst have seen the stranger knight,
    With scarf upon his breast;
He's called by lords and ladies bright,
    'Him of the Iron Crest.'

"The knight was crowned by Beauty's queen,
    And her fair hand he prest;
O tell me, maiden, hast thou seen,
    'Him of the Iron Crest?'"

"It is a strange song thou hast sung. Knowest thou the knight?" asked Donna Maria, hurriedly.

"I know him well, lady," replied Don Alfonso.

"Art thou what thou seemest?   The tones

of thy voice sound not unfamiliar," added the lady, with increased agitation.

"I am not what I seem, peerless lady,' replied the knight. "Dost fear me?"

"Nay, ask me not. I will go if thy song be sung."

"Stay, Donna Maria, stay!"

"Who art thou?"

"Let thy heart tell thee."

"Bold man."

"The bold should win the fair."

"And thou wilt say I am fair?"

"I will run a course with him who dare affirm thou art not the fairest in Spain."

"I must not hear this."

"I love thee, bright lady."

"Nay, 'tis unmaidenly to list to thee."

"Say but one word—that thou dost not hate me."

"Hate thee! I hate no person—hatred is unseemly."

"Give me but the shadow of a hope, and there is no deed I will not dare for thee," said the knight with deep earnestness.

"It cannot be," replied Donna Maria, sighing.

"Speak, dearest of thy sex—what meanest thou?"

"Listen, since it must be. Once on a bright summer day, long, long ago, when the sweet birds were singing, and the sun smiled through the clouds, another came and knelt at my feet."

The dear lady paused, and her bosom swelled with a deeper emotion than wont.

"And thou didst love the young knight

who knelt at thy feet on the bright summer day, when the birds sung, and the sun shone, long, long ago," said the knight, with strange eagerness, as he gazed upon the maiden with an expression of unutterable love.

A deeper blush overspread her beautiful visage, and her head fell lower upon her bosom as she replied:

"I loved the brave young knight, who knelt at my feet on a bright summer day!"

"Where dwells he, maiden?"

"In the regions of ceaseless summer—he died in Palestine. He went to the holy city with lords, and nobles, and belted knights, to redeem the sepulchre of our Lord. He died in battle with the Saracen, doing his devoir like one who has earned his spurs."

"And thou dost cherish his memory still?"

"And I cherish his memory still. Ask no more lest I appear forward and unmaidenly:" and Donna Maria turned away her head.

The knight buried his head in his hands, and was deeply moved.

"Am I indifferent to thee?" he said at length, kneeling to the lady.

"Nay, question me not—rise. leave me, I entreat of thee. Have I not dealt truly with thee?"

"Thou hast, by St James!" replied Don Alfonso, fervently. "I bless thee for thy candour, though it bars me from thy love. And now I have word for thy ear, and thine alone. Has Sir Haro been here of late?"

"Sir Haro was here this day," replied the maiden,

"Lady !" and the knight advanced a step, and spoke in a low voice.

"Lady ! let thy father beware of Sir Haro. He will bring no good upon thy house."

"My heart hath told me thus, noble stranger. I see him not without a sense of danger. Speak to me again of this caballero."

"Of him I can tell thee but little. He is suspected of treasonable designs. He is tampering, no doubt, with thy father's faith. God grant he listen not to him."

"What shall I do ?" cried Donna Maria, greatly distressed.

"Speak to thy father—tell him Sir Haro is suspected—that he is closely watched—that he will bring down ruin upon all who are connected with him."

"I will, generous knight. I will tell him all thou hast said and more. May it avail him much. For thy warning I will give thee kind thoughts."

"Then shall I be amply rewarded. Knowest thou Nugnez de Lara ?"

"He was here with Sir Haro. They conversed much apart, and earnestly."

"Lovest thou Nugnez de Lara ?" Don Alfonso looked searchingly at the maiden.

"I love him not."

"I say to thee—and see thou forget it not—beware of *him*. And now, lady bright, I must away; but I will see thee again. When I learn more, I will tell thee more. Till then, farewell, and may all good saints attend thee."

The knight bowed, and the porter showed him out.

The maiden had loved, and yet she sighed when he departed. How strange are the workings of the human heart. Who can account for its likes and dislikes—its antipathies and hatreds? Towards the unknown knight, Donna Maria felt herself attracted as by some incomprehensible power; from Nugnez de Lars she felt herself repulsed.

CHAPTER VII.

THE MEETING.—THE ABDUCTION.

When Don Alfonso returned to where he left the minstrel, he was nowhere to be found. He searched for him in vain—in vain he called. He saw naught save the sombre hues of night —heard naught save the echoes of his own voice. The minstrel had become wearied and gone—gone with his armour. There was no alternative—he must return to the inn in his minstrel garb. Annoyed at the circumstance, he returned to where he had left his horse. To his deep mortification his faithful steed was not there. Thinking it possible that the animal had broken his bridle and strayed away into the woods, he looked about in every direction. He was no more successful than he had been in his search for the minstrel. His horse was not restive, and so well trained that he was wont to wait his master's return with his bridle loose upon his arching neck. The knight at length abandoned the search, and pursued his way to the inn on foot.

We will now look after the minstrel. When Don Alfonso left him to enter the castle, he

stood a few moments absorbed in deep thought.
At length he started suddenly from his
reverie.

"I have it," he cried; "a thought strikes
me. I will accomplish two purposes at once.
I will forward my cherished projects, while at
the same time I punish the audacity of this
unknown adventurer."

Saying this, Nugnez de Lara—it *was* Lara—
walked rapidly down the descent. "His steed
must be near," he said, "I will look mid yonder group of trees. Ha! fortune favours me.
I see the knight's horse fastened to an elm."

Lara unloosed the beast, and mounting it,
rode to the other side of the cliff of rocks.
Having done this, he returned and secreted
himself near the drawbridge of the castle, to
watch the egress of Don Alfonso. Not long he
waited. He saw him come out—look about
him for the minstrel, and descend the cliff into
the valley. Lara followed at a short distance
—saw him search for the horse, and finally set
out for the inn.

"Now I will play thee such a trick as shall
do thee little good, proud knight of Calatrava,"
muttered Nugnez, as he ascended once more to
the castle. After a short pause, he walked
boldly to the portals, and demanded admission.

"What wouldst thou?" asked the porter.

"Tell thy mistress the Knight of the Iron
Crest would see her alone, one half hour hence,
without the walls of the castle. Let her fail
not to come, for he hath important communications to make, and to him who makes the
request time is precious. Here is yellow dust

for thee, good porter—see thou doest well my bidding."

"Well shall thy commands be obeyed, most worshipful knight. My lady, I trow, will be nothing loath to hear from so bold a cavalier, the fame of whose exploits has filled the land."

"And say to Donna Maria," added the knight, "that which I have to communicate must be said to-night, for after this hour it will avail her nought. And look thou, tell her this, that no other ear may hear, and bring me word of thy lady's reply."

The knight paced the court impatiently till the porter's return.

"What said thy mistress?" he asked.

"She will meet thee on one condition."

"What may *that* be?"

"That I attend her outside the gate."

"Nay that must not be. Our interview must be private."

"Your interview may still be private. I will stand aloof, and thou shalt speak unheard by other ears to the fairest lady in Spain. What will it matter, if so be I hear thee not?"

"Can I see her on no other condition, sayest thou?"

"On no other condition, thou of the Crest. It was long ere she would consent to this. I told her the knight was noble, and meant her no scathe, and then she said, 'Let the knight meet me in the court and I will hear him.'"

For a few moments Nugnez was silent.

"What word shall I carry to my mistress?" asked the porter.

"Tell her the occasion is so pressing, that I

will meet her as she has named; but see thou
put a goodly space between us. I will allow
no eavesdropping. Thy reward shall be in pro-
portion to the distance thou keepest. Here is
gold—thou shalt see its colour again ere long.
Just over the drawbridge, I will await thy return."

Lara walked to the spot he had designated;
the porter to his mistress. The interval of the
latter's absence to the knight seemed very long.
In a state of nervous uncertainty he paced to
and fro. His position was one of peculiar embarrassment and delicacy, when considered in a
certain light. Not only had be obtained another's armour unfairly, but his horse also.
This was not all—he was personating the suf-
ferer for a purpose most vile and cowardly, and
his heart told him so. Nugnez de Lara had
been too well schooled in the laws of chivalric
honour not to feel some twinges of conscience
at their palpable violation. He felt enough of
the meanness of the part he was acting to make
him dread detection and exposure above all
things else.

So keenly was he alive to the infamy and
unfairness of his course, that he started and
laid his hand upon his sword, at every sound
that was borne to his ears upon the fitful
breezes of the night. The fall of a leaf sent
the blood to his brow—the sound of the swaying
boughs hastened or retarded his footsteps—the
scream of the night raven caused him to pause
in his walk, or sent a cold thrill to his heart.
Once he imagined he heard steps ascending the
cliff, and his guilty thoughts told him that it was

the unknown knight returning to look for the delinquent minstrel. He held his breath in alarm, nor moved until satisfied that his fears had deceived him. At length he heard the portals of the castle thrown open, and steps upon the drawbridge. Donna Maria and the porter approached. The former advanced with trembling steps. It is true that she relied firmly upon the honour of the knight she believed herself going forth to meet, yet she consented to the meeting with the greatest reluctance. The knight of Calatrava had left her but a short time before. Why had he not communicated to her the important matters he spoke of, then ? Had he had opportunity to learn things of such interest in so brief a period ? Perhaps he had, and the information promised concerned the conspiracy, and her father's safety. How then could she hesitate ?

She went forward. The knight advanced to meet her—bowed low, and was silent. The porter at a motion from him walked away at a quick pace.

"Stay," said the lady, somewhat alarmed.

"Nay! fear not, lady-fair, there is no danger."

Donna Maria started. The voice was not the voice of the unknown.

"This way, lady—a step further."

"Nay! I can hear thee as well here."

"But other ears must not hear what I shall say to thee."

The lady suffered herself to be led or rather drawn still further from the castle.

"If thou hast aught to say I will listen to thee; if not I will return."

The knight had laid his hand gently upon her arm and exerted a gentle force which he gradually increased assuring her that no harm was intended. He now put forth a degree of strength which justly raised her fears for her personal safety.

"Unhand me! if thou art a true knight," she exclaimed in alarm; "unhand me, or I will call for help."

Lara gave no heed to her words. The lady's fears were now thoroughly aroused, and she shrieked violently for aid. The words of entreaty and fear fell upon deaf ears. The knight lifted her in his arms as though she had been an infant, and bore her swiftly down the descent. The aged porter was too far away to render assistance to his dear lady. With his precious burden, Lara vaulted into the saddle as soon as he had gained the valley, and, putting spurs to his horse, dashed away as fast as the ruggedness of the path would admit. But he bore in his arms an insensible weight—the maiden had fainted ere she had reached his steed. When she recovered, she entreated him in the most touching manner to return with her, nor persist in an act which must end in ruin to both.

"Thou art not he I had thought. Thy voice is not *his* voice. Thou art a false knight, and deserve not the honours of knighthood."

Lara made no reply. He was anxious to remain unknown to his fair captive at present, for reasons good.

"Thou hast dealt deceitfully with me—thou hast a craven heart."

Still there was no reply. Reproaches were as ineffectual as entreaties. Finding it impossible to move her captor, she vented her grief in tears and sobs.

"Thou art thwarting thyself," she said, after a little pause. "Hadst thou wooed me in knightly fashion, I might not have proved unkind. Yea, I might have learned to love thee: now thou hast put it beyond my power. I can for the future regard thee only with the contempt thou deservest."

The knight could no longer remain silent.

"Lady!" he said in a broken voice, "I have wooed thee as belted knight should woo fair maiden. My prayer arose unheeded. Thou didst hear as those that hear not, and turned away with scorn wreathed upon thy sweet lips—lips which should do nothing but smile for ever."

"Then thou art Nugnez de Lara," and the maiden wept afresh. "I scorned thee not then; but now I scorn thee from the depths of my soul. I would my scorn were a fire to burn thee, and my thoughts the lightning which blasts the overweening."

"Then thou hast thy wish, for I swear by St James, thy cruelty will drive me stark mad."

"Would I had the power to soften thy heart, instead of driving thee mad."

"The slightest accent of kindness from thy dear lips can do that."

"Not so, false knight, for I have entreated with tears, and thou didst listen to me unmoved."

"Maiden, I love—I worship thee."

"Then take me back, and I will forgive the

part thou hast acted, and lock the secret of to-
night's doings for ever in my own bosom."

"That cannot be. Ask something I can
grant thee."

"Thou canst please me in no other way."

"Then I cannot please thee," replied Lara,
sadly.

"Then speak not again of thy love, and
know that I can never, never be more to thee
than I am. There is no hope so cold and remote as that I shall ever be thine. Why then
dost thou persist in this violence? Thou wilt
bring ruin upon thyself."

"I have gone too far to recede."

"Nay! nay! thou hast not—I will forgive
the past," urged the maiden, earnestly.

"My sterner nature prevails. I will not take
thee back, until thou goest back the wife of
Nugnez de Lara."

"Then Maria de Guzman will never return,"
cried the lady, with deep feeling.

"But the wife of Lara will."

"The wife of Lara and Maria de Guzman
will be two persons. I swear to thee by the
moon over our heads, by the stars above us, and
by Him who rules them, that I will sooner be
Heaven's than thine."

"Thou wilt be more merciful anon," said
Lara, much moved.

"Never to thee."

"Force me not to be cruel, lady," he added,
in a subdued voice.

"Imagine I have repeated what I last said,
for thy answer."

"Suffering will teach thee kindness."

"Never."

The knight made no reply, but, wrapping his mantle about her, rode on in silence.

———

Don Alfonso reached the inn on foot. The next morning he resumed his journey. Before night he arrived at the valley where bivouacked the Bohemian horde.

"We are at the end of our journey," said the guide.

"I see no castle," replied the knight.

"I will tell thee a secret—the conspirators meet not always in the castle of which I spoke."

"Where meet they, then."

"In the dark valley before us there is a cavern deep and spacious. There, during the hours of night, come they to hold their meetings oft. Not far from hence is the castle of which I told thee; but if I understood thee rightly, it is not the castle that thou dost want, but those who are hatching treason."

"My eyes are on thee, thou wandering son of Bohemia; see thou playest me no tricks. And if thou deal not truly with us, we will make short work with thee."

The Bohemian evinced the same contempt of danger as heretofore.

"Talk to the wind," he replied. "It will heed thee as much."

The party soon stood at the entrance of the cave.

"Here ye will dismount, cabelleros," said the guide.

They looked at each other inquiringly.

"There can be nothing to fear from this

strange being," said Rodrigo. "Let us submit to his guidance still. Should he be wayward, I believe he is not vicious."

Dismounting, the knights followed the Bohemian. The latter lighted a torch at the fire that was blazing there, and, holding it aloft, plunged into the dark abyss that seemed yawning to receive them. On and on they wound, while the glare of the blazing brand fell with ghastly effect upon the earthly floor and the earthly walls. Damp as the breath of the tomb was the air they respired.

"I believe thou art leading us to Hades," said he of the happy hour, to the guide.

"When thy hour hath come, it shall be another's to lead thee thither," was the rejoinder of the imperturbable Bohemian.

"May it please the saints that he be more courteous than thou."

"And may the saints grant that thou mayest soon know which of us be the most civil."

"How much further wilt thou carry us, thou earthworm?"

"Art thou *afraid?*" asked the guide with a sneer.

"Not of *thee*, unless thou art the fiend. We fear not the wretched worm we can crush with our heel," replied Don Alfonso.

"The vile worm may be crushed, but beware how thou treadest upon the serpent, for it hath a venom for its destroyer."

"Thy venom is hurtless. It cannot penetrate an armour of steel."

"It can destroy thee, thou proud knight."

"Ha! tempt me not. I may forget the distance between us."

"I will quicken thy memory, that thou shall
never forget."

The Bohemian put a silver call to his lips,
and blew. Before the echoes had died away, a
score of armed men thronged the cavern, and
arose about the knight on all sides.

"We are betrayed!" cried Rodrigo. "Let
us sell our lives dearly." In a moment their
swords gleamed in the torchlight, and one of
the banditti had fallen.

"Hold!" cried the Bohemian. "No harm is
intended you. I wish only to teach your pride
a fitting lesson. Have no person in contempt
whatever may be his outward seeming, for thy
destiny may in some way be linked with him.
You perceive you are in the power of the despised and despising Bohemian. At one word
from his lips ye are dead men, and this very
moment have you cast burning scorn in his
teeth. Ye know no gratitude—ye curse those
who serve thee."

He waved his hand. The blades that had
gleamed in the dim light an instant before,
sought their scabbards, and the armed men disappeared as if by potent charm-power. The
knights regarded each other with astonishment.

"Thou art a cleverer rogue than I thought
thee. Verily, I like thee better. Thou hast
some wit—more than I had given thee credit
for," said Don Alfonso, with more respectful
tone than he had used heretofore.

"Thou shalt have more convincing proof of
my wit anon. But here is your place for the

present. Make known your wants at any time while my guests, and ye shall be served. Here shall ye await the meeting of those ye suspect."

The strange guide left them. They found themselves in a small compartment, which they had reached by a way they could not retrace. What was more, a sort of rude door was closed upon them, and they seemed more like prisoners than guests. They looked at each other as if the idea had intruded itself upon them, however unwelcome it might be. They tried the door or gate that closed the only entrance to their cell. The Bohemian had fastened it after him.

"By St Jago! if this fellow hath not made us prisoners I am greatly mistaken!" cried the knight of Calatrava. "He hath cooped us up like swine in the earth."

"He is a wayward being. Let us be patient, Don Alfonso. Thou knowest he is of strange mood; he may mean us no ill. Still, as thou hast said, this seems not unlike captivity."

"What else canst thou name it? We are trapped like a rat in this hole. Bars are drawn upon us, and we cannot go forth. We have been deceived by this cursed son of Bohemia. I will trust never again this faithless people. If they speak thee fair, they mean thee ill."

"But this knave hath not even spoken us fair. His tongue knows no courtesy. His speech is foul, and his deeds, it seems, are foul also."

After some further conversation, the knights concluded to make the best of what had happened, and having eaten of a comfortable entertainment that was brought them, they lay

down to their dreams; and in them Don
Alfonso went back to Palestine, and fought
over again his battles, and traversed the burning sands—kneeled and sighed at the feet of
his lady-love.   As for Rodrigo, he cared but
little what his fate might be.   His thoughts
were of his lost Ximena, and in his troubled
night-thoughts he gazed on her beauty once
again, and yet once again he heard the voice
which was dear music to him.

CHAPTER VIII.

SARACENA AND THE BOHEMIAN WOMAN.

WITH bosom torn by a thousand distracting
thoughts, Donna Teressa awaited the hour of
appointment with Sir Haro.   Numberless and
before unthought-of objections arose in her
mind as the time of midnight drew on.   If the
knight of the Steel Cross had aught to tell concerning the fate of her lover, why had he not
improved the opportunity he had already had?
If his designs were good, the meeting was un-
called for.   If he was base enough to destroy
her Moorish lover, he was base enough to com-
mit any act, and her person could not be safe if
she trusted herself in his power   To go forth,
then, at the lonely hour he had named—to pass
portal and drawbridge, and seek the eildon tree
—was little better than madness.   She knew,
she felt this, and yet she would keep the
assignation.

She loved, and what will woman's love not
dare!—danger, insult, violence, all.   She had
not retired to rest after her interview with Sir

Haro.   It is true, she threw herself upon her
bed, without divesting herself of dress, as the
weary night crept on; but a few moments of
troubled dreaminess could not be called rest.
Rest is a slumber of the mind—a forgetfulness
of its cares.

The sun, which had risen upon her so many
times with joy in its bright beams, came up,
but had no gladness for her.   Teressa arose,
and sitting by the ample window whence she
had looked in happier days, upon fertile valley
and rugged waste, felt the rays unheeded which
were wont to bring warmth to her cheek and
light to her heart.

A beautiful waiting-maid, whose soft cheeks
showed the deep olive brown of sultrier suns,
came and nestled down at her feet, and laying
the head-covered dark luxuriant curls upon her
mistress's knees, gazed up into her face with
her large melting eyes.

"Thou art sad, lady, and there is a deep
sigh in thy heart that would struggle up," said
the dear girl.

"And so art thou sad at times, sweet Saracena, when thinking of thy own land where
thou hadst thy early dreams and thy first sun-
shine.   Canst recollect of the people of the tur-
ban and ataghan?"

"Not much, lady fair.   I was young, thou
knowest, when brought hither.   I remember
their worship was different from thine, and they
prostrated themselves upon the earth at night
and morn, for to them it was the hour of prayer.
Still, methinks thou art right, and my people
are wrong."

" Why thinkest thou thus, Saracena ? "

" Because thou art good. But at times my heart yearns for my people, and I wander away to the burning sands, and sit at another knee, gaze into another face, and list to another voice; yet the face I view and the voice I hear is not more dear than thine."

"Wouldst thou go to Palestine, my girl ?" And the lady stooped and kissed the beautiful brow, and toyed with the beautiful curls.

" And leave thee ? "

" And leave *me.*"

" O no ! my home and my country is where thou art. Never send me away, for beside thee there is none to love me."

" Thou shalt never leave me."

"Speak it again, and I will be thy slave always. Who can serve thee like Saracena ? "

" Nay, thou art not my slave. Thou art my friend—my sister. This shall be the bond between us—thou shalt be my sister."

The fair Saracen girl nestled closer to the lady's feet, and kissed her hand again and again, and her black, speaking eyes sparkled with delight.

" This is the crowning act of thy goodness, and, deeply, earnestly the poor Saracen maiden thanks thee. And now may I speak to thee freely, as though I were indeed thy sister born?"

" Ay, speak to me freely, as though I were thy sister born," murmured the lady, while a half-conscious blush arose to lend a deeper hue to her features.

" Thou lovest."

Again Teressa blushed, and made no other reply than to kiss the Saracen girl.

"Thou lovest one of my people?"

The fair lady was still silent, nor chided her new sister.

"He is handsome and brave."

The lady looked gratefully at Saracena.

"He was at the tourney."

And still Teressa answered not.

"He has been here."

Still no reply.

"He was here last night."

Teressa toyed nervously with the jetty tresses upon her knee.

"Thou thinkest him in danger?"

The fair auditor shuddered.

"Thou hast seen the knight called Sir Haro, him of the Steel Cross and sinister look. He hath put thee in fear—he hath spoken thee falsely."

"How knowest thou he has spoken falsely?" asked Teressa, eagerly.

Saracena paused, somewhat confused.

"Wilt thou not chide me if I tell thee?"

"Never will I chide thee so hardly as I chide myself," replied the lady, in low sweet voice.

"Recently I have been often to the eildon tree thou knowest of. Ask me not why I went thither."

Saracena averted her eyes. Teressa stroked her round olive cheek with her hand, and smiled, saying:

"Fie upon thee, Saracena—I have found thee out."

" As I said," continued the confused maiden,
"I have been oft to the tree thou knowest of.
As I was on my way thither this morn, ere the
sun had risen——"

"Why shouldst thou go so early?"

"Nay, thou must not interrupt me—thou
wilt get my tale quicker. As I was on my way
thither, I met a brawny woman, whom I have
met before. She had coarse long hair, a tawny
face, and fierce flashing eyes. She is straight
as a reed, and masculine in her strength. She
hath a wild look, and talketh a wild harsh
jargon at times. I feared her at first, for she
hath a strange air, and looked at me so sternly.
I was flying away from her like a frightened
hare, when she strode after me, and seizing my
arm roughly bade me stay and fear not. I
obeyed, trembling in all my limbs. For a
moment, she seemed to take pleasure in my
fear.

"'Child, thou wert born in other land,' she
said. 'Thy face hath its rich olive from hotter
suns than those that shine on thee here; thou
art away from over sea.'

"I looked timidly up at the wild woman.
She was contemplating me apparently with
deep interest—almost sadness.

"'Child,' she continued, 'thy complexion is
like mine, and if thou wert wholly friendless I
could love thee; for the poor and despised take
to the poor and despised. Thou art comely, and
I would that thou wert a daughter of Roma,
but thou art too tenderly reared to learn our
wild and wandering habits now. Thou art a
busno—thou wert born over sea. Wouldst

F

thou return again to thy land, and dwell with the worshippers of the prophet?'

" 'I could not return, weird woman, for my heart is with my lady,' I replied. My fears had vanished.

" 'Is thy lady like me?' she asked, with a strange smile.

" 'O no, my lady is not like thee, for she is gentle and comely.' I answered.

" 'And I am ugly and savage,' she added quickly. 'Thou sayest well, thou from over sea—thy mistress is not like me. more than the hawk is like the pigeon. Yet she is a woman, and so am I; she might have been thy mother, and so might I. There are some pulses that beat in unison in all human bosoms; there are none so bad that they have no good, and none so good that they have no bad; I love those of *the blood*, but I hate the Gentile of every land and name.'

" 'Dost hate me, woman?'

" 'No, child, I hate thee not, and yet the law of the Calees teaches me to hate thee. Thou seemest not like a busno.'

" 'Lovest thou not my lady?'

" 'I hate her not, and that is much. But it is of her that I would speak. Tell her that her lover is not in danger—that he is not in the power of Sir Haro. He is free as air.'

"The weird woman paused, as doubting whether to tell me more. She seemed struggling with her better feelings

" 'Thanks, thanks, my good woman! I cried. 'I will tell my lady all thou sayest.

" 'I had thought to tell thee more a moment

since, but I will not tell thee. My mood has
changed. What thanks should I get had I revealed to thee all I know of what is before thy
mistress? None—none!'

" ' Speak, I entreat of thee, if thou knowest
aught concerning my mistress!' I cried, grasping
her brawny hand, and pressing it with both of
mine.

" ' Thou wert ready to fly from me a moment
ago, as from the presence of the fiend; now thou
clingest to me as if I were a princess. 'Tis thus
with human beings—they fly from those who
cannot serve them, and kneel to those who can
do them good. Thou showest the selfishness of
all.'

" ' Nay, I plead not for myself. I kneel for
another; and if thou knowest aught that con-
cerns the safety of my dear lady, tell me, as thou
hopest for pardon in the last hour,' I said, plead-
ingly.

" ' What would it avail that I should warn
thee that danger is before her thou lovest? She
would rush into it the same. It is written thus.
She would not shun the danger that lurks in
her path.'

" ' She will—good woman, she *will!*' I urged.

" ' I tell thee she will not.' replied the woman,
sternly. 'Can I not read *baji?* Thy mistress
will come here this night. Yet for thy sake I
will tell thee, for thou are swart like a gitana,
and of a pleasant countenance. Thy mistress
hath an appointment here this night, and she
will be true to her word. She will come hither
at deep midnight. alone, and yet not alone; **and
her trust will be betrayed. I have said.'**

" The weird woman was silent.

" 'And what will betide her here?' I asked.

" 'No matter—suffice it there is danger for her, and she will meet it and feel it when it is too late to recede.   Thy mistress hath a daring spirit, and she believeth not in *la bahi*.   As for thee, thy fortune shall be changeful at first, but bright in the future.'

" 'And what of my lady?'

" 'Like thine, her fortune shall be dark at first.   She hath a cup of bitterness to drink, and its taste is in her mouth even now.   When this is drained to the very dregs, greatness, and power, and happiness, such as seldom falleth to the lot of woman, shall be hers.   The bitter and then the sweet—the darkness and then the light.   Black clouds herald the storm, and fierce light-nings the thunder.   So everything has its her-ald, and wise is he who can read the heralds of life's future events.   To me the heralds of com-ing events are as palpable as yonder castle, or the sun in the heavens—for to me and my peo-ple is it given to read *baji*.   I have done.   Re-turn to thy castle, and tell thy mistress of the weird woman, with the hair like a horse-tail, and she will laugh at thee for thy pains.'

" 'Nay, my lady is gentle, and of a kindly heart.   Go with me, and she will reward thee for thy knowledge.'

" 'Yes, her servants might loose the dogs upon me   Knowest thou not that my people are hunted like wild beasts?   They have no rest in the city, in the valley, or on the mountain where dwells the Gentile.'

" 'I will drive this dagger to his heart who

dares let loose a dog upon thee, were it the last
blow I should ever strike !' I cried, passionately
grasping the dagger beneath my mantle. The
stern dark nature of the female seemed to melt,
She seemed on the point of straining me to her
wretched bosom.

"'Thy hand would make poor work with the
dagger. Thy feeble strength would speed it
but a short way towards the heart,' she said,
sadly, and in a gentle tone that sounded not
unlike thine own at times.

"'Thou art a woman,' I continued, 'and
between woman and woman there is ever a bond
of sympathy. Come with me. I will give thee a
home. Thou shalt lay aside those wretched
rags, and those raven-dark locks shall be
combed out, and thou shalt look like what thou
art.'

"'It cannot be, simple child. Thy people
would curse me for an evil hag. There would
be rebuke and blow for the uncanny woman.
My destiny is to wander among these hills.
The days of my weary pilgrimage will soon be
told, and I shall rest with those whose hope is
in the grave. My dwelling shall be in the cliffs
of the valleys and the caves of the earth. I am
not that which thou art, nor can be. The life-
line in my palm is not as that in thine. The
path of my feet is wayward and wild. I am of
those who wander in darkness, and die in the
fastnessss of the hills. My home and my grave
shall be in the fastnesses of the rocks.'

"'Nay, follow not these wild imaginings.
Thy brain is warped. Come with the Saracen
girl, and she will be thy friend.'

"'Girl, between us there can be no sym
pathy. Our paths will diverge for ever. To
morrow will widen the distance and the day
following will see the gulf still greater, as to
day sees it wider than yesterday. I thank the
for the kind words thou hast spoken, and fo
them I will serve thee in the dark hour. I have
power over thy destiny thou little dreamest
This hour hath determined me to exert it fo
thy good. When thou art in grief, and there i
none to help thee, come thou to this tree. Ant
now adieu, thou of the olive skin and the kindly
voice.'

"The weird woman drew her tall figure t
its proud height, waved her skinny hand, ant
walked slowly and majestically away towan
the mountains."

Saracena paused, and looked intently at he
lady. There was a long silence. Donna Ter
essa seemed lost in thought.

"What thinkest thou of the weird woman?"
asked Saracena, at length.

"I have but little faith in her warning. St
hath wrought upon thee," was the reply.

"I half believe her," replied Saracena.

"I know thou dost. She said truly whe
she told thee I should disregard thy warning.'

"Thou wilt not venture to-night, my lady?"

"I shall keep my word, as the sibyl hath
said."

"Then may the saints defend thee. for I fe
that there is danger for thee beneath the eildo
tree, at the hour of deep midnight, with th
sinister knight."

"I will dare it."

"The very words of the weird woman. She hath said some truth. My faith increases. I entreat of thee not to keep the appointment. Or if thou goest, let thy servants go with thee."

"Urge me not, my girl, the conflict between duty and prudence has been severe. Try not to change me now, for the Rubicon is passed. I must abide the consequences of my decision. If I have been rash, I must reap the fruits of my rashness."

The conversation was dropped for the present. Saracena saw that her words made no impression, and hoped that a more favourable opportunity might occur before the hour of assignation should arrive.

The sun mounted to mid heavens—it sought the regions of the west—it waned—it sunk behind the hills—twilight came, and night followed on its track. Despite her resolution and firmness, the heart of Donna Teressa faltered more than once. The words of the uncanny woman, and more than all, the warning of her Moorish lover, rang in her ears. The night fell darker than usual. The wind sighed about the castle with a hollow moaning sound. The shutters rustled in the aged casements, and occasionally drops of rain fell upon the windows.

"It is a dreary night," said Saracena, nestling close to her mistress.

The lady shuddered as she replied, with affected indifference:

"The wind shrieks mournfully, I will allow."

"Yes, and look—how dark! I should not

like to ɔnture forth on such a night," added
the girl

"N∘ʋ to meet thy lover, Saracena?"

The girl blushed.

"I said not I had a lover."

"Neither dost thou affirm thou hast not."

"Thou wouldst scarcely believe me if I
should."

"Nay, thou canst not evade me. Thou art
fairly caught. Wouldst thou not go forth to
meet thy lover, were the night ten times darker,
and the rain fell ten times faster, and the wind
shrieked ten times more fiercely, if his safety
depended upon the act? No confusion and no
evasion; answer."

The beautiful Saracen girl put back the
glossy curls from her brow, and raising her
large black eyes to the face of her mistress,
said, in low earnest tones, while her features
were deeper hue than olive:

"Were the night twenty times darker, fell
the rain twenty times faster, shrieked the wind
twenty times more dismally, I would go forth,
if he were in danger."

The lady caught the dear girl to her bosom.

"Bless thee for thy words, my own sweet
sister! Thou hast spoken as maiden ought,
and thou hast confirmed me in my purpose.
Wilt tell me of thy lover? He should be
noble indeed to be worthy of thee."

"A princely youth came with the brave
Moorish knight," replied Saracena, hiding her
face.

"What sayest thou? Do I hear aright? Ah,
thou rogue—thou hast stolen away the heart of

my lover's page, and kept it all from me! Fie,
fie, thou artful!" And again the white fingers
of the lady wove themselves among the jetty
curls flowing over her bosom. She loved her
fair favourite better, I trow, for what she had
heard. Here, then, was a fresh bond to link
them together.

"Our destinies shall be indissolubly linked
henceforth, and our thoughts shall be as the
thoughts of one person." And there was an in-
terlacing of arms, a meeting of lips and bosoms,
and a prolonged silence.

Hours of the dark night wore on, and nought
was heard save the beating of hearts and the
sound of respiration within the quiet chamber
of Donna Teressa.

"It is time for me to go forth," said the lady,
at length, putting Saracena gently from her
bosom.

Saracena unwound her arms and raised her
head slowly from the bosom on which it lay so
lovingly, as if afraid it might never rest there
again. Without a word she helped to array her
mistress to go forth.

When she had done so, she threw a mantle
over her own shoulders.

"Why dost put on thy mantle?" asked
Teressa.

"To assist thee," she replied.

"Nay, thou must not venture forth on this
dark night. I bid thee stay."

"I must disobey thee in this. If there be
danger it will be happiness for me to share it
with thee."

"But I command thee to stay."

"I will not leave thee, even if thou shouldst be angry with me," replied the girl, clinging to the mantle of her lady.

"Well, thou shalt go then, and may God guard thee, though harm come to me. I would not that the winds should blow too rudely upon my sweet flower, transplanted from the holy land. It has grown so well and bloomed so gracefully under my care that I fain would cherish and shield it now from frosts and winds. Now come, and let thy steps be gentle as the fall of the snow, for all eyes are slumbering within."

Arm in arm, with steps that waked no sound, the two maidens stole from the castle. The porter was sleeping. The donna took the keys softly from his girdle. She placed one in the lock, where it required all her strength to turn it. She succeeded at last, and the massy bolt flew back. With their united strength the gate swung upon its hinges. They closed it softly after them, and laid the keys down upon the outside. The lady trembled violently, and leaned against the wall for support.

"Wilt thou go back?" said Saracena, in a low voice.

"Not until I have kept my promise."

The drawbridge was down, and they passed over with fearful step.

"This way—this way," said Saracena, "and may all good saints assist and defend us."

"They will—they will," faltered the lady. "I go forward with a just purpose and a guileless heart, and whatever may happen this night, do thou believe and know that God will protect me. All will yet be ordered for the best."

"May it be the will of the saints. But here is the tree. How terribly dark—how the wind moans!" replied Saracena.

"O, 'tis very fearful. Let us kneel and invoke the protection of the saints."

The maidens knelt down upon the wet turf, and with arms interlaced prayed the protection of the virgin and all good angels. They had not risen from their lowly attitude when a man in mail stepped from the other side of the tree. The maidens sprang up simultaneously, and shrank closer to each other. The man advanced, and the maidens instinctively drew back.

"Thou art not alone," said the man, in a whisper.

"My friend is with me," faltered Teressa.

"The appointment was alone," added the man in mail.

"Blame her not that she came not alone. I came because she could not hinder me." said Saracena.

"Let thy friend leave thee but a moment, for what I have is for thy ear, lady;" continued the man.

"Step but three paces from me, sister," said Teressa, tremulously.

"Not one step I tell thee. I will not leave thy side but by force, and let him force me away if he dare," cried Saracena, clinging still more tenaciously to her mistress.

"She will not leave me. Speak what thou hast to say, Sir Haro, and I will go hence. What of the knight thou didst speak of?"

"Since it must be that thy little friend will
not leave thee, I will even whisper it in thy ear."

The supposed Sir Haro approached.

"Not so near; I care not if this maiden
shou'd hear. No nearer, upon thy knighthood
I charge thee stand aloof."

The man advanced, and with one sudden
movement threw his arms about Donna Teressa.
The ladies shrieked in a frenzy of fear, and
Saracena clung to her dear mistress with the
energy of despair.

"Come and take away this creature," cried
the man in a gruff voice.

Instantly another person made his appearance, and with a brutal oath tore the girl away
from her lady. A third ruffian led forward a
horse of mighty proportions, and the villain
who held Teressa in his arms leaped into the
saddle with his fair burden.

With a snort and a bound the gigantic steed
swept away. His comrades, mounting hastily,
followed. Saracena was left insensible upon
the earth. How long she lay there she knew
not; but when she recovered she lay in the
skinny arms of the weird woman. She opened
her eyes languidly. She saw the wild female
and the early morning.

"What has happened? Where am I?" she
asked.

"Well mayest thou ask, thou from over sea.
Thou art beneath the eildon tree, and in the
arms of the evil hag," replied the moody woman.

"Where is my lady? How came I hither?"

"Thou didst walk hither, and if thou

wouldst know aught of thy lady, ask those who know. My brain is warped, and I know nothing. Thou believest not in *la bahi*, and thy mistress laughed at idle tales," replied the woman, ironically.

"Ah, now I bethink me. I came hither with my lady. Where is she? Evil hath befallen her."

"Thou believest not in the ravings of the evil hag."

"I believe all—everything—what thou wilt; only tell me of her I love," cried Saracena, falling upon her knees.

"Thy mistress, child, is far away with the uncanny people."

Saracena paused, and seemed recalling her thoughts.

"Didst thou not say to me that I might seek thee in the hour of danger?" she asked.

"I said that thou mightst seek me in the hour of danger," replied the woman.

"To me that hour is now. I appeal to thee for aid."

"What! to the evil hag?"

"No, not to the evil hag, but to thee."

"How can one like me help thee, the beautiful and tenderly reared? Does the chicken seek aid from the hawk, or the lamb from the wolf?"

"Do I not obey thee in this?"

"What wouldst thou?"

"Take me to my mistress."

"How can I?"

"I know not, and yet I have **faith in thy** power."

The woman was silent.

"Thou shalt go to thy mistress," she said, at length. "Canst thou ride?"

"I can do anything for one I love."

"Then come with me."

Saracena arose and committed herself to the guidance of the Bohemian woman. Leaning upon her arm, she walked with difficulty away toward the broken country. They entered a thick wood. Saracena's strength began to fail. She sank down to the earth, saying, "I can go no further." The Bohemian woman lifted her tenderly in her arms, and bore her on. There was something strange and contradictory in her manner; with all her rudeness there seemed mixed a touch of kindness—a gentleness with all her harshness.

"I shall weary you, good woman," said the girl.

"That will be nothing new. I have wandered in weariness all my days. My way is a weary way. What matters it to thee? Who will be the less happy if my old bones ache, and my strength faileth?" she answered, sharply.

"Speak not thus, good mother, for it gives me pain. I will be sad when thou art weary—I will grieve when thou art in sorrow."

"Will that soften my lot? Will that assuage the hunger pangs, or quench the fires in my brain?"

"I will give thee gold."

"Will that make me blithe—will that bury the memory of the past—will that make thy people love the evil hag? No, no, believe it not!" said the woman, bitterly.

"What can I do for thee," sobbed Saracena, "to reward thee for this kindness?"

"Nothing, child, nothing now; but when thou canst serve me, I will tell thee."

They had now reached the thick wood. The woman paused before a rude hut, from whence a smoke issued. Pushing open a crazy door, she entered with her burden. In a corner was a mattress, and she laid her carefully thereon.

"Rest thyself here for a short time, and then I will take thee to thy mistress."

Saracena was weary indeed, and needed rest. Having drank of a cordial which the weird woman had urged upon her, she sank into a troubled sleep, and, dreaming, turned restlessly and moaned.

CHAPTER IX.

XIMENA—PRESENTIMENTS—THE DEATH.

TROUBLED were the thoughts of Ximena, as she lay down to rest on the night preceding the fatal combat. A nameless fear oppressed her. A premonition of an unhappy morrow brought unwelcome dreams. That which was to be— the thing that was written—had cast its shadow. It is often thus when evil is hanging over the path of human destiny. The mind hath a vision of tears, and a glance at the coming sorrow. It may invoke the aid of reason and philosophy, but both fail to do away the impression that Heaven would make. When the Power that made us speaks, let none refuse to hear.

Ximena would have banished the nameless

dread, but a will higher than hers had sent it, and she had no power to drive it hence. From a restless dream she was aroused by the sound of a minstrel harp. Her heart told her who was at the window. She arose and looked out. The deep voice of song was borne to her ears, It smote like a dirge upon her heart. What meant her lover ? "

> " The good steed that bears me
>   Is saddled in stall—
> By the hand of Rodrigo
>   Lozano shall fall."

Why sung he, 'neath the window of his lady, words of such singular import? She listened more intently, and the shadow fell more darkly upon her heart. The nameless fear assumed a more tangible form. The "coming event" took its proper shape.

"Ximena! Ximena! 'tis night in Castile,
But 'tis day to the darkness thy spirit shall feel—
When waking from slumber thou hearest with dread,
Lozano is sleeping the sleep of the dead."

Fearfully palpable was the danger that threatened. There had evidently been a quarrel of a serious nature, and the affair was to end in blood. Her lover and her father were involved in the quarrel, if the language of the song would bear a literal interpretation. It ceased, and she heard her lover depart with slow and sorrowing steps. Her heart told her he had gone to return no more. She turned

from the window, and knelt low at the image
of the virgin, and felt at that moment, that she
had lost a father or a lover —perhaps both. The
next few hours would determine. She could
not doubt that which Rodrigo had sung had a
deep meaning. She flew to her father's cham-
ter, but he was not there. She passed rapidly
through the different suites of apartments. He
was not within ; and with livelier fears she re-
returned to her own chamber and knelt again
before the virgin.

She resolved to seek her father on the first
appearance of daylight, and if possible prevent
the meeting. She passed a sleepless and anxious
night. As she was preparing to put her plans
in operation, she heard an unusual commotion
in the hall among the servants. Wild with
fear, she flew rather than walked thither. The
servants were running to and fro. A leech and
several knights were seen in a group at the extreme end of the hall. Ximena by an irrepres-
sible impulse rushed towards them. They gave
way in surprise as she approached. What a
fearful sight met her vision ! Pale, bloody,
mute, motionless, dead, lay the once proud
figure of her father stretched along the floor.

With piercing shriek, which rang out like
the shrill scream of the night raven, she threw
herself upon the body, and her hair was drag-
gled in her father's gore. The next moment
she was borne away as insensible as the corse
itself.

Little by little her waiting maid made known
to her the particulars of her father's death.
The grief of Ximena was deep, and greatly

aggravated by the circumstances of her father's unhappy end. With sorrow unfeigned she followed him to the family vault, and saw his cold ashes deposited with those of his ancestors. In one fatal night she had lost a father and a lover. Grief indeed! How could she unite her destiny with one whose hand was red with her father's blood? Was it not sinful, ay, almost impious, to suffer her thoughts to dwell upon him? Great and painful was the warfare in her breast.

"Thou sayest my father dealt the aged Vivar a blow?" said Ximena to her waiting-maid, the day after the funeral rites.

"He dealt the father of thy lover a disgrace-ful blow," replied the maid with a sigh, and kissing the hand of her mistress.

"Was there no remedy for this but blood, Zara?"

"My lady, there was no remedy for such insult but blood; and the aged Vivar was too old to hold the lance and sword."

"Could not Rodrigo avoid the meeting?"

"Thy lover could not avoid the meeting without deep stain to his knightly honour. Who but the son should avenge the father's wrongs?"

"What will the world say of this act?" inquired Ximena, earnestly.

"The valour and filial piety of Don Rodrigo are in the mouth of all. They say he hath done well his devoir in avenging his aged parent," replied Zara.

"Say they so? Surely thou art jesting with my sorrow."

"I tell thee, my lady, that all Castile rings with the praise of Don Rodrigo Parents hold him up as a pattern to their sons, and say, ' Be thou like the son of Vivar.' Thy lover hath done only what the laws of chivalry hath forced him to do. Why shouldst thou hate him?"

"I hate him not; I cannot hate him. I have tried in vain to do so: and yet he hath slain my father," sobbed the sorrowing maiden.

"That was his evil fortune. He deplores the necessity that called him forth, as deeply as thou, and hath gone hence to fall by the hand of the Infidel Moor ; for he said, ' What is life without Ximena? There will be no music in the song of singing birds, and no sweetness in the waters of the murmuring streams.'"

Ximena smiled.

"Thinkest thou he will perish by the hand of the Infidel? " she added.

" He went hence in such a pitiful state that he cared not longer to live. He will fall in battle, doing great deeds, for he is the doughtiest youth in Castile. What need that thou shouldst lose a father and a husband at the same time?"

"'Thou reasonest strangely, Zara," sighed Ximena.

"And do I not reason rightly, dear lady?"

"Perhaps my heart might say thee yea, while duty might admonish me to say thee nay."

"Dost thou not love him, my mistress?" said the faithful creature.

"I love him most dearly, Zara."

"And thou mayest do so without sin," rejoined the girl, "for so saith a holy friar this day."

The countenance of the peerless Ximena brightened, and she half smiled through her tears, to hear her lover exculpated from blame, and to hear it said that she might love him without guilt. She spent the day in deep thought. She seemed meditating some great purpose—something that would require all her energies.

"Zara," she said earnestly, "my lover must not perish. I must and will save him."

"How canst thou save him? Ere this he is doing battle with the Infidel. He will be found where the fight is thickest."

"What maiden has dared can be dared again. I have heard of ladies going forth in disguise to find and aid a lover," answered Ximena, with a searching look at her maid.

"I have heard of such things, and read of them in the books, but methinks it would be a wild and dangerous enterprise. One might fall into the hands of the banditti, or the wandering people (gipseys). What remedy would there be for such a sad mishap? The brigands might slay one alive."

"A love which will risk nothing is worth nothing. What is a love that will make no sacrifice and incur no danger? The one who would accomplish much, must dare much. Everything has its price, and love has its offerings and sacrifices."

Wild and incoherent were the dreams of Ximena that night. She formed a thousand plans to save her lover. Early in the morning she sent for her father's page.

"Order two of the best steeds from stall,

and then come to me with a suit of thy
clothing. I have a purpose which I will tell
thee anon."

The page bowed and withdrew to fulfil his
mistress's commands. He brought the suit of
clothes as desir-d, and again withdrew.

Laying aside her costly robes, she proceeded
to put on the garments of the page. To her
this was an awkward and unwonted task, and
she made her toilet with difficulty. It was
completed at length, and she stood before her
mirror a very handsome page. She contemplated herself for a moment, and then sitting
down, covered her face with her hands, and
wept bitterly. She felt the rashness of the act
she was about to do, and the construction her
conduct might bear. She might be thought
unmaidenly and forward, and even wanting in
respect to the memory of her dead father. She
recovered her calmness at length, and rang.
The page made his appearance. Ximena blushed
crimson, and Jean, the handsome page, was
embarrassed. To see a pretty woman in such
guise was to him a novel sight, and yet he
thought he had never seen her look more inter-
esting.

" Where are the servants, Jean ? " she asked,
with some confusion.

" In the hall and kitchen, my lady," replied
Jean.

" Thinkest thou we can get egress without
being discovered ?"

" I think we may, lady."

" Dost thou love thy lady, Jean ? " she continued.

" Heaven knows I love thee dearly," cried
the page, kneeling at the feet of his mistress.

" Wilt thou go with me and be my protec-
tor ? "

" I will go with thee to the world's end—to
death, if need be," he replied with fervour.
" See ! my arm is not so weak as it might seem.
I could fight in good battle for lady fair."
And Jean drew forth his sword, and held it up
in the sunlight, and fenced about the room.

" Thou wilt make a valiant knight, I doubt
not. Thou hast not a puny arm as thou sayest,
and thy steel is of goodly length. Thou shalt
be my champion."

" And I will endeavour to deserve the honour."

Ximena put a purse of gold beneath her
girdle, and with Jean made her way to the
court by the most unfrequented way. They
reached it without being discovered. Two
noble steeds were there saddled and housed.
Jean assisted his mistress into the saddle, and
then mounting the other horse they galloped
away.

" Mend thy pace," said Ximena to the page.

Giving the steeds spur and reign, they dashed
through the streets like the wind, and were
soon galloping without the walls of Castile in
the open country.

" Whither wilt thou go now, my lady ? "
asked Jean.

" I scarcely know whither I would go," she
replied with confusion. " Let us proceed in
the direction we are now journeying, and after-
wards we will determine upon the matter."

"I read thy purpose, lady," said the page, modestly.

"Tell me, then," Ximena replied, with a blush.

"Thou wouldst see thy lover."

"Who taught thee to read?" murmured the maiden.

"Thy confusion and blushes taught me to read what I have said."

"Then thou must look on me no more, for thou wilt know too much."

"Nay, I cannot turn from thee. I am happy only when I gaze upon thee. Thou wouldst rob me of my happiness."

"The young tongue hath learned flattery already. What wilt thou be when older?"

"Truth is no flattery, lady mine—"

"Worse and worse. Thou wilt say many gallant things to thy lady-love, when a belted knight."

"Now thou are flattering. Do not make me love thee better."

"Jean, thou lovest me not."

"My lady, I would die for thee?"

"Then thou thinkest I would see **my** lover?"

"I do, in good sooth."

"Why should I see Rodrigo?"

"Because thou thinkest him in danger."

"Would it not be unmaidenly for **a maiden** to go forth thus, thinkest thou?"

"Not to save a lover in despair."

"Then thou dost not reproach me, Jean?"

"I reproach thee! Far be it from me. Thou **art** doing only what other maidens **have done.**

It is a generous and noble sacrifice thou art making."

"Thank thee, Jean. Thy faithfulness will avail thee much. I will buckle on thy armour when thou art knighted."

They kept on at an easy pace till noon, without meeting with adventure worth relating.

"I see a man yonder in palmer's weeds," said Jean. "Let us approach him, and it may be he can tell us of the knight."

The palmer paused, and observed them attentively as they advanced.

"Hail, pilgrim!" said Jean.

"Hail, thou page, and a fair day to thee!" replied the palmer, crossing himself, devoutly. "Whence comest thou?" he asked.

"We come from gallant Castile, good pilgrim. Thou art from the tomb of the Christ, and the sands that burn, I trow?"

"I am, courteous page; and it is a weary way. But he who wanders for his sin, must heed not the sultriness of the sun, or the weariness of the way. He who sacrifices to the Lord must bring an offering without blemish. The firstlings of the flock are his. Were the way to the sepulchre paved with sapphire, and thou couldst journey thither in a chariot of beaten gold, thy offering would not be acceptable to the Lord."

"I doubt thee not, thou bearer of palms. Heaven is pleased with our self-denials, and our mortifications of the flesh, I trow," answered Jean.

"Whither are ye journeying?" inquired the palmer, with a searching look at Ximena.

"We are travelling towards Leon, whither the noble knight we serve has gone. Hast thou seen a knight upon the way, in dark-brown mail and plate, with a towering crest and a goodly presence, with a squire of gallant bearing?"

"Three days ago I saw the knight you describe, and he was attended by a sullen Bohemian and a swart woman," replied the pilgrim.

"Which way went they?"

"They journeyed yonder towards the hills. A goodly distance is between you. They are far in the mountains, toward Sierra Morena ere this. Thou wilt need whip and spur to overtake them. There are banditti in the wilds and woods whither thou art tending—fear ye not?"

Again the eye of the pilgrim rested attentively upon Ximena.

"I never was taught to fear, palmer," replied Jean, proudly.

"Thou art a gallant and well-spoken youth, by all the saints! Fortunate is the knight who hath such pages as thou and thy friend."

Ximena felt her face glow, and bending forward to the saddle-bow, affected to adjust her bridle rein.

"Whither goest thou, thou pilgrim with the staff?"

"I go to the mountains to fulfil a vow, and I would gladly journey in thy fair company."

"Thou shalt go with us with right good-will, and thou shalt show us the way whither the knight went. The steed that bears me is

swift and strong, and my weight is nought.
Do thou mount with me. It will rest thy
weary limbs. We will be of mutual advantage
to each other."

The palmer mounted with the page. As
they went on, a wild being met them. Her
hair was braided with mountain broom, and
the valley flower lay upon her faded and sickly
cheek. The wandering woodbine was wound
about her waist, and the amaranth was in her
bosom. She sang in a voice cracked and
wild:

" He sleeps! he sleeps! but they say he's dead,
    And they say that his dreams are o'er ;
And they have raised a mound above his head,
    And think he will wake no more.

" They say that the sleep he is sleeping now
    Is the dark and final rest ;
And they say that the coldness on his brow
    Is the coldness that death impressed.

" And they say that I am a moon-struck one,
    And my senses have wandered away ;
But I only watch for my sleeping son —
    He will wake with the early day.

"And they say that I must not wander and
        sing,
    And sleep on the mound at night ;
But a mother's love is a sleepless thing,
    And my boy will awake at light.

" But I heed them not, for I know he's asleep,
    And I know that he soon shall wake—
And the icy spell that is on him now,
    The light of the morning will break."

"She's crazy," said the palmer, when she had ceased.

"Come with me," she said, "and I will show you where he sleeps."

They turned their horses' heads whither she pointed, and stood beside the new made grave. The skinny faded creature was Mina. The son of Sir Haro had been laid away there to moulder in obscurity and neglect, as he had lived.

"He had a deep wound upon his head, but it will be healed when he wakes," she said.

"Who gave him the wound?" said the palmer.

"A wicked knight in black armour wounded my boy. May the evil demon smite him!"

The palmer started, and looked with pity upon Mina. He put his hand beneath his woollen garment hastily, and drew gold therefrom, and threw it to her. She gathered it up with childish eagerness, saying, "I will keep it for my handsome boy when he awakes."

"Let us go hence, in the prophet's name! I would look no longer upon this poor creature."

"Thou art a comely page," she said to Ximena, and laughed strangely. "But thou art not used to hardship and danger. Return—return! Wild and weary is the mountain way, and the wandering people are abroad" And again the poor creature laughed close in the ear of Ximena. Her words and air had a strange significance.

"What is thy name?" she asked.

"Alvarez," replied Ximena, with an effort.

"Ha! that was my boy's name. Wait here till he wakes and thou shalt see him."

Advancing close to Ximena, she spake in a whisper, "*Beware!*"

The maiden started as if a serpent had stung her. Had the crazy being guessed of her sex? It would seem so, from the remark she had just made; and like the palmer, Ximena was anxious to move on. When they left her, she was singing in a shrilly voice—

"He sleeps! he sleeps! but they say he's dead,
And they say that his dream is o'er;
They have raised a mound above his head,
And think he will wake no more."

"Poor creature!" said Jean; "she will watch long for her boy to awake, if the black knight sped the blow that sent him hence."

"Who is this black knight of whom so many speak?" inquired the palmer.

"Would I could tell thee. Thou art not the first that hath put the question. There are many knights in Castile that would give their best steed from stall to know. He is the flower of chivalry; but none know whence he came or whither he went. He hath been seen several times in these parts. He rises up when least expected, like a thing uncanny, and departs as mysteriously as he came. It is believed that he wooeth Donna Teressa, the sister of Don Alfonso, and kinsman of Ferdinand. Moreover, he is an Infidel."

"A wonderful being is this Moorish knight," answered the bearer of palms. "Fearest thou not he will rise in thy path?"

"I told thee, good pilgrim, that I never was taught to fear. Were he before me now, I should not fear him.   It is unknightly to harm a page."

"If he be so terrible and uncanny, he would heed little the laws of chivalry.   I dare say he would cleave thee from chin to chine with his ponderous battle-axe," rejoined he of the escalop shell.

Ximena shuddered, and looked furtively about to see if the dreaded apparition was not near

"I think he would not harm a page," she said.

"Why thinkest thou thus, handsome Alvarez?" asked the palmer, with a smile.

"Because he is brave, and the brave scorn to take advantage of the weak and defenceless."

"Thou sayest well, Alvarez, but this knight is an Infidel."   And the pilgrim looked intently at Ximena.

"That matters not.   Knightly honour is the same in all countries.   The brave, of whatever name and creed, are noble and generous," she answered, warmly.

"Who learned thee such doctrine as this?"

"Nature taught it me, good pilgrim."

"Then nature hath taught thee a good lesson, Alvarez.   The saints grant that thou mayst never forget it.   Upon the long and ofttimes weary pilgrimage of life upon which thou hast entered, it will avail thee much.   It is a thing which hath entered into the philosophy of few. Human understanding is usually bounded by different views."

"The views of the multitude have little to do with the truth of a theory," replied Ximena.

"Very true. Thou speakest with the wis
dom of riper years. Thou art a strange page
Hath thy master more like thee?" There was
something peculiar in the tones of the pilgrim.

Ximena could not command the blood tha
rushed to her face. She felt it tingling there
as if it were coming through.

"Thy fingers are not used to the bridl
rein." he continued.

"He hath been ill of late," said Jean
quickly, "and he hath barely recovered. H
hath been long within doors."

"That will account for it," rejoined th
palmer. "and yet his cheek hath the hue of
health."

Again the maiden felt her cheek burning
Fortunately for her their attention was arreste
at that moment by another object. A tall wo
man, with a flashing eye, stood suddenly in
the path before them. Her dark locks fell in
disordered and tangled masses over her tawny
bosom and neck. She folded her gaunt arm
upon her breast, and manifested no dispositio
to move on as they advanced.

"*La buena ventura*," she cried; "let me tel
the *buena ventura* to this fair company,"

The party drew up. The wandering wein
woman fixed her eyes for a moment on th
pilgrim and the maiden. "Stretch forth thy
hand," she said to Jean. "There is little upo
thy palm, as yet; thy way hath been ver
smooth; and thine hath leen a spring o
flowers. The future for thee hath something-
something of joy, and something of woe. Le
thy hand be upon thy sword when thou win

est the mountain way, and be thou courteous to men of God, and those who wander for their sin. Look thou never behind thee in battle, and when thou strikest. strike to the heart. Thou wilt make a bold knight, should Heaven lend thee length of years."

She turned to Ximena.

"Thy hand, fair page, with money to cross thyself with."

Ximena hesitated, saying, "I care not for the *buena ventura.* good woman, but here is the money with which to cross thyself."

"Nay, but I must view thy palm."

The maiden stretched out her white hand. and the wandering woman held her taper fingers in hers, wrinkled and dry.

"Thine is as comely a hand as ever grew to the body of page," said the weird woman; "thy palm is as soft as is the palm of lady-fair, and the fingers as delicate as woman's; thy service hath been light, and thy master indulgent. One would think thou hadst oftener held the needle than the stump. I see here the lifeline, and it is deeply traced, showing thy position will be a prominent one, and thy days many. Here are the shorter lines running transversely, standing for the respective years of thy pilgrimage. They commence here, with these first lines for infancy and childhood, counting this way as we grow older. I will number them. Thou art older than thou seemest, or there is no truth in my art; thou art sixteen. according to the lines, and yet thou seemest but ten. The sixteenth line almost crosseth the life-line, which shows that thy life

will be in danger. I bid thee beware of the
sixteenth year, for therein there is danger for
thee to shun, and according to the reading of
thy fortune, it is close upon thee. Beware of.
rugged passes and lonely wild wood, for thou-
knowest not what may be here. I advise thee
to keep in the path that turneth to thy left, for
him thou seekest hath gone thither. Be courteous to pilgrims;" and the wandering woman
glanced meaningly at the palmer.

"And now mine, said the pilgrim, as the
woman turned away.

"Thy fortune is already read; it is written
upon thy brow; thou wilt make thy fortune
anywhere."

The pilgrim held out his hand.

"'Tis a mighty hand," said the weird woman, "and might well hold the lance; there
is power in thy palm; thou art one born to be
obeyed. There is some spot on earth where thou
art supreme, and thy voice is as the voice of
Heaven; thou wouldst be safer there than here,
and yet thou art safe in all places. Thou art
ever in the midst of danger, and still thou art
safe—thou art a favoured one, and bearest a
charm with thee always." And then, in a low
voice, "Attend thou to the safety of this page,
for his hand hath grasped seldom the stirrup,
or held often the rein."

They exchanged glances, and the wandering
Bohemian woman went her way.

The day wore away; the sun was declining
behind the hills. The party were wending
slowly through a lonely pass. The faint rays
of the dying sunlight threw an additional

gloom over the wild scenery, and struck a deep
dread to Ximena's heart. The dark forebodings which had haunted her imagination
hitherto, assumed a more terrible form. A
sense of evil so acute in its nature grew upon
her, that from every bush or frowning rock, or
overhanging cliff, she expected to see some horrible figure start with uplifted hand. A vision
of the wandering people arose, and she saw herself borne rudely away to wilds unknown, dishonoured and shamed. She shuddered, and
drew closer to Jean and the palmer. The sun
went down, and the darkness settled more
heavily in the pass. There was a sound of
coming feet, a clatter of hoofs, a wild cry,
and the party were surrounded by a band of
brigands.

"Down!" cried the palmer to Jean; and in
an instant Jean slid from the horse, and as
quickly the bearing of the pilgrim changed.
He sat firm and erect in his saddle, and his
countenance was terrible to look upon; the fire
of battle gleamed from his eyes; he reined the
mighty horse with a magic hand; and from beneath his palmer's gown he drew a sword of
fearful length.

"Hence, ye craven-hearted villains!" he
cried, in a voice which made the boldest quake;
and pressing close to the side of Ximena, he
cleft the arm from the shoulder, through plate
and mail, that was laid upon her bridle-rein.
Down came again his ponderous steel—down
through helm, and skull, and visor, and gorget,
and there was a riderless horse flying through
the pass, with mane erect, distended nostrils,

E

and fiery eyeballs turned sidelong toward the light.

"Have at you again!" he thundered; and, darting amid the score of ruffians that pounced upon him, another and another bit the ground, and other saddles were empty, and other steeds riderless. His sword rang upon the helmet of a gigantic brigand, and broke at the hilt.

"He is gone!" shrieked Ximena, as she saw him weaponless. "Now may the virgin protect him."

Before the words had died upon her lips, the palmer had snatched a ponderous battle-axe from the saddle-bow of one of the ruffians, and, grasping it with both hands. he fought like a lion, and cleared for himself a bloody arena. The noble horse leaped from side to side, or bounded forward, to favour his blows, as if rider and beast were governed by the same impulse. While the palmer was thus engaged, doing nobly his devoir, another of the brigands pressed towards the maiden. Jean saw the movement, and, dashing like lightning from the side of the lady, buried his sword in the horse's flanks, and horse and rider rolled upon the earth.

"Curse thee for a young satan!" cried the balked bandit; and, extricating himself from his dying steed, he rushed upon Jean. The bold youth recoiled not at his approach.

"Now, leave thy mistress's side, or by S James I will cleave thee from chin to chine!' he cried, in a voice hoarse from passion.

"Thou shalt walk over my body ere thou lay thy hand upon her!" he exclaimed, fear lessly, while his features glowed with indignation.

"Then take this!" and the bandit raised his sword to strike. Ere the blow fell, the terrible battle-axe of the palmer shivered his skull, and scattered his brains upon the rocks. The brigands had fled—the pilgrim was master of the ground, and Ximena was saved from — she scarcely knew what; the peril of that hour had passed. Ximena had nearly fainted with fear when she saw the danger of the faithful page; and pressing to her side, the doughty palmer supported her in his arms. She soon recovered, for the maidens of that period were inured to scenes of blood.

The palmer now caught one of the riderless steeds, and mounting, the party moved hastily on, for fear the brigands might again return.

The maiden was conscious that her sex was known to her deliverer, although he had not alluded to the subject. She felt grateful for the kindness and delicacy of the unknown. It is true he wore palmer's weeds, but he was evidently a knight of great prowess and rank. And the dark sayings of the weird woman occurred to her mind, and lent mystery to the pilgrim. He was in her idea a hidalgo born, and from him she had nought to fear, but on the contrary, was safe under his protection. She thanked her deliverer warmly for his timely aid, and prayed that the saints and his lady bright might reward such valour.

"I am already rewarded," replied the pilgrim, in most courtly style, and bowing low.

" My reward is here; " and he laid his hand
upon his heart.

She gave him an approving smile.

"And to thee, Jean, I owe a debt of gratitude for your fidelity and bravery," she added,
turning to the page.

The conversation was turned by Jean's ask-
ing the palmer how far it might be to an inn,
or if he had any knowledge of one in the
vicinity.

"There is none within a half day's ride,"
replied the palmer; "but a ride of two hours'
will carry us to an old castle, of which tradition hath not been silent. If it be thy pleasure
we will travel thither," he answered, looking
at Ximena.

"Let us go to any place where we can find
anchor, be it hut or castle." she replied.

The parties now went forward at a rapid
rate, and had but little opportunity for conversation. Two hours' hard riding took them to
the castle. It was the same we have visited
before, in company with Sir Haro and other
knights. Its grey walls and falling towers, as
seen in the moonlight, offered but a cold welcome to the benighted travellers. No lights or
watchfires gleamed a greeting from the lofty
battlements or the crumbling terraces. An air
of grand and still desolation was over all, and
Ximena shuddered at the sound of her own
light footsteps upon the drawbridge. The crazy
portals creaked mournfully, as though sighing
for their former lord and their past splendour.
Like all earthly things, this great monument of
human labour was passing away.

The weary steeds were lightened of housing, barding, and bit, and suffered to provide for themselves. The party entered the dreary hall. It was still and breathless, like the dead. Its darkness was as the darkness which shall close over us all—even the darkness that shall shut down upon us in the land whither we are tending. No porter showed the way, and the voice of greeting had died long ago in that old hall. By dint of much exertion a fire was lighted upon the long-deserted hearthstone, and its warmth seemed a mockery of the tomb.

CHAPTER X.

THE KNIGHT OF CALATRAVA AND THE BOHEMIAN.

THE next morning the Bohemian did not make his appearance, nor did he until the hour of noon. Their fare, however, had not been of the most homely kind. Considering all the circumstances connected with their situation, they had but little reason to complain in this regard. When the hour came I have named, the eccentric guide made his appearance.

"We have waited thee long, thou most wayward," said Don Alfonso. "What news bringest thou?"

"I have no news, hidalgo. I came to conduct thee to the castle. The conspirators will not meet here as I expected. For some reason they have changed their plans. I will show thee to the castle, and then my duty will be done. Your steeds are waiting," replied the Bohemian.

"Thank the saints! Let us away from this den with all convenient haste," answered the knight.

The knight and the squire followed the guide to the open-air by the same winding way by which they had entered, and mounting, pricked away after the Bohemian with right good-will.

They pressed on for about an hour, before any adventure occurred worthy of note. They had just entered upon a level plain, when their attention was arrested by some object in the distance. As they went on, it assumed the out-lines of a tent, and such it proved to be.

"Some knight is desirous of doing a feat of arms. I see his shield hung up without the tent. Let us read the heraldry displayed thereon."

"A knight is desirous of performing a pas-sage at arms for his lady-love, and for this pur-pose has he come hither under a vow. He is called the Knight of the Crescent. He will joust as follows—viz., the knight that is van-quished in the encounter shall do the bidding of the vanquisher for a certain time, which time shall be the term of five months. If the Knight of the Crescent shall be overthrown, he will obey the bidding of the knight who shall over-throw him—if, on the contrary, the knight with whom he shall joust shall be overthrown, the knight shall do the bidding of the victor. The Knight of the Crescent will joust on these con-ditions, and on no other, for thus hath he sworn to do for the love of fair lady, and he asketh this favour of all noble knights and hidalgos who shall pass this way."

"This knight would perform a strange passage at arms," said he of the happy hour.

"Singular, but not unheard of," replied Don Alfonso. "I will help him to fulfil his vow;" and with his lance he touched the shield. Instantly a knight sprang forth in costly armour, mounted on a powerful Arab steed. The knight's armour was a plate of polished steel, which flashed in the sun, although there was no vain attempt at ornament.

His baldrick and belt were plain, though of the best material, and his sword hilt and scabbard were of pure gold, but the hilt bore not the form of the holy cross. The crest of his helm was a crescent, and proclaimed him an Infidel knight. He was followed by a page of matchless symmetry of person and beauty of feature.

The Knight of the Crescent bowed to the Knight of Calatrava, and in courtly phrase thanked him for the favour he was about to do him. Wheeling their horses they galloped away in different directions, and turning, bore down upon each other with lance in rest. Terrible was the concussion. Their lances were shivered like reeds. New weapons were brought, and each knight "on God and on his lady called."

Each felt the necessity of putting forth his prowess, and exerted himself to the utmost. Their steeds sprang forward like lightning. If the shock had been terrible before, it was now doubly so. The lance of Don Alfonso was shivered to splinters, and he himself forced from his saddle to the ground.

The Knight of the Crescent leaped down from his horse, raised the visor of Don Alfonso, and assisted him to rise.

"I hope so noble a knight is unhurt," said he, courteously.

"I believe I am unhurt, save my pride, although thou hast given me a fair fall," he replied, with a smile.

"Then thou hast suffered but little, for thou art of too valiant a heart to let a single overthrow grieve thee. I have heard thou hast never yet been fairly vanquished, thou of the Iron Crest. Never before ran I so fierce a course—and never before had I a lance shivered upon my crest."

"I cannot grieve that I have been overthrown by so noble and fair-spoken a knight. Thy courtesy makes me half forget that I have fallen," answered he.

"Now, by the Koran! thou dost outdo me in courtesy. Although chance hath given me the advantage in this encounter with lances, yet hath it given thee the mastery in greatness of mind and knightly courtesy. I half regret thou hadst not been the victor," retorted the Knight of the Crescent, warmly.

"Enough, generous knight, enough," cried Don Alfonso, in a voice from which all traces of disappointment or chagrin had vanished. "If thou hadst not fully subdued me with thy lance, thou hast now done it with thy generosity. I am fairly vanquished, and according to thy conditions wait thy bidding."

The Knight of the Crescent drew a ring from his finger and showed it to the Knight of Calatrava.

"When I shall send thee this ring, whether thou be at the tourney, in the field, at church, or at the altar, thou shalt leave all and follow the bearer without delay or questions," he said, bowing.

"When thou shalt send me the ring," replied Don Alfonso, "whether I be at the tourney, or in the field, or at the church, or at the altar, or at lady's bower, I will leave all, and follow him who brings it without delay or questions."

With many gallant speeches they parted, and the Knight of Calatrava rode on. The Bohemian loitered a moment after the knight had departed.

The Knight of the Crescent spoke in a low voice.

"Lead the knight by the longest and most difficult way, and make many idle delays that I may gain time. I will be on the way anon. Haste thee on, lest the knight should look back and see thee speaking with me."

The Bohemian nodded in his usual sullen manner, and rode slowly on after the knight.

"Come on, thou laggard," said Don Alfonso. "The grass will grow beneath thy horse's feet."

The words fell unheard or unheeded. The Bohemian kept on at the same pace for a few moments, and then stopped.

"Why art thou stopping?" said tne knight, impatiently.

"I was considering which will be the shortest way," he answered, ungraciously.

"If thou meanest to consider the remainder of the day, we will dismount, or move on and find the way ourselves."

"As it may best please thee," replied the Bohemian, indifferently.

"Thou art most obstinate."

The guide heeded not the last remark, but seemed in deep thought.

"We will go this way," he said, at length.

"And thou wilt take us the longest way, or I am no Christian," answered the knight, tartly.

"Thou canst go the other way if thou wilt, thou of Calatrava. It may be thou wilt like it better," was the moody rejoinder.

"We shall do nothing with this fellow if he has not his own way," said Rodrigo.

They travelled for about an hour over a road rougher than any they had hitherto seen.

"This son of darkness is a malicious villain. He taketh pleasure in leading us into difficulties. We are no sooner out of one trouble than he involves us in another. He brings us nought but vexation," muttered the knight.

"Let us be patient," replied the squire.

The cabelleros now struck into another path. They had gone but a short distance when they perceived a man walking before them.

His dress was of singular style, and was wild and disordered. Long white hairs flowed down over his shoulders, and he carried in his hand a wand. He went slowly, and stooped as he walked, pausing occasionally, and looking steadily at the ground.

"A strange being seems he before us," said he of the happy hour.

"It is the wandering seer," replied the Bohemian. "He hath the gift of second sight

He can read *baji* better than my people. The
spirit of *Undebel* (God) or *benjui* (the devil) is
strong upon him. He is seen in the wildest
places when the storm is fiercest—upon the
summit of the beetling cliff, or the brink of the
dizzy precipice, and far up on the overhanging
mountain top. When his long grey locks
stream wild in the wind, and the lightning
flashes in his old eyes and the thunder breaks
in his ears, and the rain beats upon him, he
mutters strange words, and shakes his wand.
'Tis then his vision is keenest, and the future
is spread out most plainly before him. When
he hath had a vision of what is written, he hath
no rest until he hath spoken."

"Believest thou in this?" asked the knight.

"I believe what I know," replied the guide.

"Thou mayest safely do that, son of Bohemia. But hast thou known him speak the
truth?"

"I have heard him speak oft, and I never
heard him speak false. If he telleth thee aught
thou mayest believe it sooth, and write it down
as a part of thy life, though the vision be not
for many years," rejoined the guide solemnly.

"I perceive thou art deeply tinctured with
superstition of thy people," answered Alfonso.

"Were yonder old man there, with the white
locks, and the wand, to tell me to turn my
horse's head to the place whence we have come,
and his tail to the place whither we go, and
leave you to keep your own good company, I
would do so," replied the Bohemian earnestly,
and in a low voice.

"Is thy faith, then, so deep as this? I pray

he may not bid thee turn back, for it is now we
need thy service.   Tell us something wherein
his words have proved sooth ? "

"Rein up your steed, and I will tell you one
thing ere we overtake him of the strange spirit
and the uncanny lore.   See ye forget it not."
The Bohemian rode close to the knight, and
lowered his voice almost to a whisper :

" I and my brother were journeying through
the most lonely passes of La Mancha.   We had
been in high spirits during the day, and unwound the dismal way with blithe hearts, nor
dreamed of danger near.   When the sun was
highest in the heavens we met yon old man.

" He was in his wildest mood, and the second
sight was strong upon him.   He looked steadily
at my brother, and such a look !   May he never
gaze at me thus.   He raised his wand and spake
in a hollow voice :

" ' The sun has gone down, I see two horsemen in a gloomy pass.   I hear a death-stroke,
and my old eyes see an empty saddle and a flying steed.   Let those who journey towards the
west turn back towards the sunrise.'   The old
man ceased, and looked upon the ground.   My
brother shuddered like one cold, and turned
pale.

" ' What sayest thou, old man ? ' he gasped.

" ' Didst thou not hear me ? ' he said sternly.
' I told thee I heard a death-stroke, and saw an
empty saddle, and a riderless steed flying away
like mad.'

"The seer again waved his wand, and walked
slowly away.   My brother was silent and sad,
I rallied him on the impression the seer had

made, but failed to bring back his cheerfulness. Seeing that his sadness was real, I proposed retracing our footsteps, but to this he would not listen, for he scorned to be thought a coward. The sun set darkly. We had kept up a forced conversation for the last hour, but now it flagged, and we rode on in silence. We were in one of most the horrible passes of the Sierra. My brother was a little in advance. A troop of Spanish brigands sprang from the tangled thicket near us. One stroke of a sabre clove his skull. His horse dashed away at full speed. I turned and fled for life. Fortunately I was well mounted, and escaped after a hot chase. Since then, I have heeded the words of the wandering wizard, and believed when he shook his wand."

"Thou hast good reason," said the knight, in an altered tone, "if thou has spoken truly."

"The book of thy Christ is not truer," he replied.

With pleasure the Bohemian perceived that his tale had made an impression. They were now close upon the seer. He had stopped, and was looking intently upon the ground.

"What seest thou, thou man of the gray locks?" asked Alfonso.

The person addressed raised his head slowly, and looked at the speaker.

"Well mayest thou ask," and pointed to the west with his wand. "I saw that which concerneth thee much."

"Tell me thy vision quickly, for time presses. Here is yellow dust to sharpen thy old eyesight."

The seer looked scornfully at the knight. With his wand he sent the gold ringing away among the rocks where no eye might find it.

"I care not for thy gold. Thinkest thou my power can be purchased with such dross? I have a knowledge which all thy gold cannot buy, and yet thou wouldst prize that knowledge more than all thy dust."

"How then shall I get the knowledge you speak of?" replied the knight, more respectfully.

"Listen to me, nor deem my words the ravings of an old dotard. Last night at the set of sun, I sat upon the highest peak of yonder mountain, and looked down a thousand feet towards the rugged rocks below, where a hundred cataracts dash their spray. The blood grew hot in my bosom, and my old eyes were strong in their second sight. I saw pictured in the misty spray, that arose from the eddying, boiling waters beneath, a knight in dark brown armour, with haughty crest. He stood, or seemed to stand, near the draw-bridge of a castle, and a lady-fair was with him half fainting and trembling. Suddenly he raised her in his arms, and dashed down the cliff whereon they had stood. A gallant steed was waiting at the foot of the declivity, and he vaulted into the saddle with the fainting fair. In another moment, I beheld them sweeping away through the dark night. On, on, rode the knight through wild and wood. He drew up at castle gate, but no porter came forth to open, or bid them "come in," and they entered a castle hall, but it was warmed by no fire. and lighted by no lamp, and they were greeted by no lord or lady."

The seer ceased, and shook his wand again towards the west.

"What meanest thou, old man?" cried the knight, earnestly.

"I mean as I have told thee. If thou art wise thou wilt understand. The way is before thee. Shouldst thou find a castle that is lord-less, and a hearthstone that hath no fire upon it, remember what the old man said to thee on the winding way. And list! Wert thou to search the old ruin, thou wouldst find in an apartment as lone as a corpse in its winding sheet, a broken image of the virgin. Thou knowest that the old castles of feudal lords were built in troublous times, and have secret ways and sliding panels, which have been used oft for various purposes. Much hath been overheard when those who spake deemed no ear was listening. I have said enough. The ear that is open, and the heart that hath wisdom, will dwell long upon a word, and profit thereby. Words oft have mystic meaning, which become palpable as dwelt upon. Farewell! Forget not the knight in the dark brown armour, with the haughty crest."

The seer turned away, and was going.

"Stay! strange old man, stay! Thy words interest me," cried the knight. "Speak yet again, and let thy words be more apparent."

The seer turned upon his heel.

"I will speak once again, and then thou shalt hear no more from me. When the knight in dark brown armour bore the lady away from the castle, a minstrel was walking lone and disappointed towards an inn in a contrary direction."

The seer turned for the last time, and was soon lost to view.

"What canst thou make of this?" said the knight to the squire.

"I can make but little of it. I should pronounce it a disconnected harangue without meaning."

"I agree not with you," replied he of Calatrava. "I believe it meaneth much. But what thinks the son of Roma?" he asked, turning to the Bohemian.

"To the son of Roma," said the Bohemian, "it is as plain as a written book. To him each word hath a meaning."

"Then read to me the riddle," replied the knight.

"Thy heart hath read it to thee already. How couldst thou fail to understand? Knowest thou a castle upon a cliff?"

"Right well."

"And a lady?"

"Ay!"

"Knowest thou aught of a minstrel, and a knight in brown armour?"

"Something of this kind, I know. And as I think of it, my mind is filled with strange misgivings. As thou sayest, his meaning is evident, but the tale may be an idle one to work upon my fears."

CHAPTER XI.

DON LOPEZ AND LARA.

DON ALFONSO mused upon what he had heard until at length the whole assumed a tangible form. In spite of his efforts to the contrary, the tale of the wandering seer filled him with apprehension. Some evil—if the seer could be trusted —had befallen Donna Maria, and the precise nature of that evil had been defined. Moreover, she had been carried to a deserted castle. As the Knight of Calatrava reflected on the matter, his fears for the safety of Donna Maria gathered new force. It was not strange that he resolved to satisfy himself of the truth of what he had heard by a visit to the castle of Don Guzman, towards which they were now journeying. Arrived there at nightfall they found all commotion. Groups of peasants were gathered within and without, talking earnestly.

"What has happened?" asked the Bohemian.

"Thou hast come recently to these parts if thou hast not heard," replied the peasant addressed.

"Thou art right. We have but now come hither from a wild part of the country."

"The country must have been wild indeed, if ye heard not the news. The daughter of Don Lopez de Guzman hath been forcibly carried away, and no one knoweth whither."

"Know they not who hath done this?"

"A certain stranger knight, known as the Knight of the Iron Crest, hath borne hence the daughter of Don Lopez de Guzman."

" What dost thou say, knave ?" cried Don Alfonso.

" What I say," replied the peasant, " I say boldly. A stranger knight, but lately from the holy land, hath forcibly abducted Donna Maria, the daughter of Guzman."

" Thou liest, villain!" shouted the knight, in a rage. " A thousand times thou liest. Repeat thy words and I will trample thee into the dust. The knight of the Iron Crest is before thee."

The peasants drew back, trembling at the words of the knight.

" Restrain thy anger, sir knight. Let us learn more of these peasants," said Rodrigo, and turning to them, he asked in a mild voice:

"What hath been done to recover the lady?"

" Much hath been done. Don Lopez de Guzman hath offered his daughter's hand in marriage to the knight who shall rescue her from the power of the villain, and bring her back safe."

Don Alfonso drew his good sword, and holding it aloft, swore by its crossletted hilt, never to rest until he had wrested the lady from the false knight who had borne her hence, and he called on Heaven to record his vow.

Don Alfonso and his squire regaled themselves on the good cheer of the innkeeper. They suffered their steeds to take the rest and provender they needed, and mounting, pursued their way. They had gone but a short distance before they perceived several persons on horseback pricking rapidly towards them. As they drew nearer, they proved to be Lopez de Guzman and Nugnez de Lara, attended by their squires. They rode furiously, and drew up their steeds by the side of Don Alfonso with such force as nearly threw them to the ground.

"Art thou called the Knight of the Iron Crest, and late from Palestine?" asked Guzman, in a stern voice.

"I am called the Knight of the Iron Crest, and am lately from Palestine," replied Don Alfonso, courteously.

"Then thou art a false knight, and I charge thee with forcibly carrying hence my daughter," retorted Don Lopez.

"And I charge thee with the same crime, and am here to prove it upon thy body," added Nugnez de Lara.

"I swear by the holy cross, I am not guilty of this baseness," replied Don Alfonso, holding up his sword hilt.

"Upon thy body I will prove thee a false knight!" rejoined Lara, fiercely, throwing down his glove.

"Nugnez de Lara, I accept thy guage, and am ready to prove my innocence in mortal combat. May God speed the right. But to thee, Don Lopez de Guzman, I swear by my knightly honour, that I know nothing of this matter more than what I have learned within the hour. I was now hastening to offer my services to thee, that the guilty one might be brought to punishment and thy daughter rescued."

"Wast thou not at the castle on the night of the outrage?" asked Lara.

"I was there on that night!" answered the knight of Calatrava.

"Thou seest he does not deny being there,"

added Lara, to Don Lopez. "Thou wilt mark that."

"Didst thou not go thither in armour?" he continued, turning again to Alfonso.

"I went thither in armour!" he answered.

"And didst thou not leave thy horse in the valley near the castle?" still questioned Lara.

"And I left my good steed in the valley, near the castle, but mayhap thou canst tell better than *I* who took him hence."

"Thou hearest, sir knight," Lara resumed, "that he denieth not the matters whereof I have questioned him. So far, all corresponds with what the porter hath said. We cannot doubt the guilt of this unknown person, who hath the audacity to call himself a knight."

Don Alfonso turned proudly to Don Lopez.

"I was at thy castle," he said, fearlessly, "on the night on which Donna Maria was abducted, and I went in armour, but not for the purpose whereof I have been most unjustly accused. I blush not to say I went thither to get speech with thy daughter. At thy gate I met one in minstrel garb, with minstrel harp. I exchanged my armour for his minstrel habit, for I was desirous to be unknown. I bade the minstrel await me at the portals. When I returned he was gone with my armour. I searched in vain for him, and called aloud. Descending to where I had left my horse, that had also gone. I was forced to reach the inn on foot. Not until within this hour, knew I what took place on that night, or what use was made of my armour or my gallant steed. I call on Heaven to witness that I speak the truth."

The words seemed to make an impression on Don Lopez, which Lara perceiving, hastened to efface.

"Thou seest, noble Guzman, that this tale hath been cunningly wrought for the occasion. His guilt and falsehood in this matter are but too palpable."

"I swear upon this cross, that the noble knight, my master, speaketh the truth," said Don Rodrigo, riding close to Guzman, "and I am ready to make good my words upon the body of any knight who dare gainsay me."

The squires of the knights who were hidalgos, and right gaily attired, now rode haughtily forward, eager to dispute the matter with Don Rodrigo at the point of the lance.

"I will joust with ye both one after the other," cried Rodrigo, eagerly, "and brand me a liar if I bring ye not both to the ground; but first, we will attend to our masters."

Don Alfonso and Lara now prepared themselves for the combat. A spot was soon found suitable for the encounter.

"Now may God adjudge the cause between ye," said Guzman, as they fixed their lances in rest. They spurred on their horses, and at the first course the lance of Alfonso was driven through the helm of Lara, and he was borne to the ground.

The knight of Calatrava leaped from his horse, and placing his foot on his fallen foeman, drew his dagger.

"Now, confess that thou hast done me wrong, or thou hast not a minute to live," he cried, in a terrible voice.

The stout heart of Lara quailed.

"I have done thee wrong," he said, faintly.

"I give thee thy life. Ho! attend to thy master," said he to Lara's squire, and stooping, unloosed the visor of the knight. There was a slight wound upon his head, otherwise he was little hurt.

"Now thou shalt try it with me," said Rodrigo to Lara's squire, when his master had revived. "If God helpeth the right, I will leave thee in a worse plight than thy master."

So saying, they mounted their gallant steeds. The animal of Rodrigo was of Arab breed, and swift of foot. He ran the course with such impetuosity, that his adversary, together with his horse, was overthrown, and sorely wounded.

"Confess now that thy cause is unjust," said Rodrigo, putting his foot upon his adversary's breast, as his master had done with Lara. "Confess thy cause unjust, or I will slay thee here without fail, and without mercy, for thou hast brought this quarrel upon thyself."

"I yield," cried the squire, in a voice more feeble than his master's had been, for the lance of Rodrigo had pierced his cuirass; and left a wound upon his breast.

The squire of Don Guzman preferred to decide the matter with the battle-axe. They fought on foot with that weapon, and so skilled was Rodrigo in the use thereof, that he brought his antagonist to the earth at the second blow. So hardly was he dealt with, he was borne away insensible.

Now, Rodrigo had seen but sixteen summers, and they all acknowledged that he had done nobly his devoir, for the other squires were much older.

Don Alfonso turned to Don Lopez, saying: "Thou hast greatly wronged me in thy heart, in charging me with this grievous misdemeanour, Sir Guzman, for I am innocent as I have heretofore affirmed. Nevertheless, I forgive thee, and attribute thy belief rather to the insinuations of a villain, and a false knight, than to thy heart. I have sworn before I had met thee this hour never to rest till I had found thy daughter, and I here renew my vow."

Bowing low to Guzman, the knight of Clatrava galloped away. The Bohemian was the last to follow. As he turned, he said to Guzman in a low voice:

"Nugnez de Lara hath carried away her thou art seeking."

The words of the Bohemian were overheard by Lara, and he rushed towards him with uplifted battle-axe, crying in a voice hoarse with passion:

"I will dash out thy brains, thou vagabond son of Bohemia, and give thy lying tongue to the crows."

The Bohemian laughed sneeringly, and putting spurs to his horse, flew away in an instant beyond his reach. Lara cared not to follow him.

The parties now rode rapidly toward the ruined castle. It was past midnight when they entered its gloomy gates. Everything about the castle served to recall to Alfonso's mind the words of the seer. It was evidently the place hinted at by him. What had been told him had thus far proved true—although by what

means he had obtained his knowledge he knew
not.

Here, then, he might expect to find—if the
man of second sight could be further trusted—
the lady of his heart. She was doubtless im-
mured within these damp and cheerless walls.
But how should he prosecute the search?
Where should he commence? It was now the
hour of deep darkness. With no torch to guide
his steps, how should he thread the intricacies
of the castle? The knight of Calatrava paced
the hall, while Rodrigo and the Bohemian lay
down and slept. When the early light had
come, Alfonso commenced an examination of
the ruins. He sprang with unfaltering speed
from room to room. Mouldering doors cracked,
which had not swung upon their hinges for
many years, and rotten boards, which had not
been pressed by human feet for time unknown,
shook beneath his heavy tramp. He heard a
footstep behind him. He turned—the Bohemian was following.

" The broken image of the virgin ! " he said,
significantly.

The words of tne guide recalled those of the
seer.

" Knowest thou aught of the room in which
the old man saiu there was a broken image of
the virgin ? "

" I have alreaoy found it," he replied.

" Let us to it, then, in the virgin's
name ! "

The wandering Bohemian led the way. In
a few moments they stood within the apartment where we left the palmer sleeping.

"There is the broken image!" said the guide.

The knight of Calatrava paused, as if recalling his thoughts. He repeated the words of the seer :

"The castles of the feudal lords were built in troublous times, and have secret ways and sliding panels, which have been used oft for various purposes."

"There must be a sliding panel here, or the seer hath spoken falsely," he cried. "Let us press upon the walls, and examine them attentively."

They did so, but no secret spring was found. The knight began to despair of success. The man of second sight was some impostor who would fain play with the credulity of the credulous. Thus far, however, everything had corresponded with his words. He had resolved on one effort more, when his attention was called by a cry from the Bohemian.

He looked—the secret panel was found. The guide stood beside it with his usual indifference. The knight stepped quickly into the passage. The darkness at first was too great for any object to be seen distinctly, but his eyes soon became accustomed to it, and he was enabled to see on the floor a folded paper He took it from thence and leaving the passage, opened it. Within it was a ring of great value. The missive ran thus:

"*To the Knight of Calatrava* :

"When thou hast found this paper, place the ring within upon thy finger. When this is done, procure a torch, and with cautious feet unwind thou the secret way. Let thy steps be light, for the structure beneath is treacherous. As thou goest, feel before thee with thy good sword. When thou art far down the narrow passage, thou wilt find two diverging ways. Take thou that upon thy sword hand. And now move on more silently and carefully, for there is more than one danger to dare. Thou wilt not fear for thy hand is strong, and thy cause just, and at the worst the ring will save thee. Go on until thou standest upon the ground. Walk straight before thee for a few paces, and then turn to thy bridle hand, and see thou makest no sound, and let thy breathing be soft. See that thy feet stumble not— that thy armour give no ringing noise. It may be thou wilt hear voices and see the glimmering of lights, but heed them not. When thou hast passed these, there will be one more turn, and that will be to thy sword hand. Thou wilt now come upon a man who guards a door. He will start to his feet in surprise, and demand thy business; but ere he hath time to wind the horn at his side, do thou show him the ring upon thy finger. His manner will change, and he will speak thee fairly. Say to him—

" 'Thy master has sent me hither to take from hence the lady. Show me to her quickly.'

"He will hasten to obey thee. When he hath done this, bid him take thee to the court of the castle by the shortest way. When thou hast reached the court with thy fair charge, thou wilt mount her upon a swift horse, and away to her father's castle. Fail not to let thy gallant squire tarry at the ruins, and fail not to place the ring that hath served thee so well upon his finger. Bid him, the coming night, be in the secret passage near the room in which is a broken image of the virgin. In a closet within that apartment thou wilt find food. When thou hast reached the castle of Don Lopez de Guzman, thou wilt demand the hand of his daughter in marriage, for thou lovest her well.

"Thou needest to hear no more. A thousand years of life and happiness to the Knight of Calatrava."

The amazement of the knight cannot well be conceived when he read this strange paper. It was doubtless the work of a friend—but what friend, and how did he arrive at this knowledge? How singular was the tone of the entire missive! Yet it had an air of deep truthfulness and sincerity.

"Wilt you entery on dark place?" asked the guide.

"I would not fail to do so for the crown ot Ferdinand," replied Alfonso, earnestly.

"Then thou wilt need a torch, for it is darker than the bottomless abyss," and the Bohemian walked away with wonted sullenness of manner.

"Thy squire is still sleeping," he said, when he returned. "Is there nothing thou wouldst have him do?"

"Ay, thou hast spoken in good time. Hasten and bid him have our steeds in readiness in the court, and there await my coming."

The Bohemian did as he was bidden.

"Shall I lead the way?" he asked.

"Not for the world. Give me the torch," he replied, "and do thou follow noiselessly."

With careful tread the Knight of Calatrava went forward according to his directions. With one hand he held aloft the flaming brand, and with the other he grasped the hilt of his trusty blade, and felt the way before him.

Though his step was steady, and his arm was strong, and externally he was calm, his heart was full of tumultuous thoughts, thoughts of which the reader can scarcely dream.

CHAPTER XII.

DONNA MARIA.—LARA.—THE INTERVIEW.

We return to Donna Maria. When we left her, the knight, Nugnez de Lara, was bearing her away through the dark night. Before morning he drew rein at the ruins. Dismounting, he wound a small horn which he had worn at his belt since he had changed his minstrel garb for warrior harness. A short pause ensued. The tramp of armed men was heard who filed rapidly into the court.

"I would see your leader," said Lara.

The athletic villain with whom the palmer had fought, stepped forward. Rude greetings passed between them.

"What wouldst thou, noble Lara?" asked the bandit captain. "All here is at thy service, as thou well knowest."

"I would have thy best accommodations for this fair lady, who much needeth rest and food."

"Follow then to the home of the fearless and free."

Half fainting with fear, the fair lady was half led, half borne, through a narrow way which seemed to wind downward without end. They reached at length the bandit home. It consisted of one capacious apartment, and several smaller ones, variously disposed. One of the lesser compartments was assigned to Maria.

"Let her be attended to the best of thy ability, as befits her rank; and, dost hear? let her be well guarded, for she came not altogether by her own will," said Lara.

"Thy wishes shall be obeyed. She shall have the best the castle affords, and one of my knaves shall keep guard at the door. I perceive thou hast lost nothing of thy gallantry, noble Lara. I foresee that thou hast agreeable business on thy hands. I wish thee success," replied the bandit.

Refreshments were brought to Donna Maria by a withered beldam, but she put them from her, saying, "Leave me. Since thou canst not give me liberty, I want nothing else. I would be alone."

Solitude brought troubled thoughts, but even these were less painful than when in the presence of Lara. The indifference which she had hitherto felt towards him, had within the last few days ripened into positive aversion. She knew him to be head-strong and violent, and knew not to what extremity he might proceed. She was now among creatures of his own, completely in his power, with little to hope, everything to fear. One thing, however, she was resolved upon—never to become his wife,

and never to survive her honour.   She drew a
dagger from beneath her mantle, where she had
placed it previous to her meeting with Lara,
and placing it in her bosom, she said, "This
shall serve me in the hour of need."

The night was spent in mournful anticipa-
tions of what the light might bring.   The next
sun might set upon her a shamed and dishonoured thing.   And with these reflections was
mingled a thought of a gallant youth who knelt
at her feet on a bright summer day, long, long
ago ; and she wandered away over burning
sands and swelling waters to Palestine, and
saw him kneeling at the Saviour's shrine, and
then doing deeds of arms in the battlefield upon
the bodies of the Infidel Moors.   The vision
went still further ; she saw the youth who had
kneeled at her feet on a bright summer day,
wounded to the death, bleeding and dying, and
trodden to the dust by the iron hoofs of barbed
steeds ; and she wept for her lost love who
perished in holy land.   Incomprehensibly
blended with these reminiscences and thoughts,
was the Knight of Calatrava.   Her love had
been given to another, and still her heart told
her she was not indifferent to him of the Iron
Crest.

How was this ?   The question was vain—
the matter quite inexplicable.   She found herself utterly incapable of explaining the exact
state of her feelings.

Early in the morning she was notified by the
old beldam that Lara would visit her.   This
was no agreeable information.   She was not
kept long in suspense.   He soon made his ap-

pearance. Maria stood face to face with the only being in the world she detested.

"A good morning to thee, fair lady," said Lara, bowing.

"Nay, it is the foulest morning that ever dawned upon me," replied the donna, with disdain.

"Say not thus, queen of my soul," responded the knight, fervently.

"I repeat it a thousand times. Never dawned so foul a morn on Maria de Guzman."

"Then listen to me, and to-morrow thou shalt say, 'Never a fairer sun hath risen upon me, for it hath never before risen upon me the lady of Lara.'"

"Were I the lady of Lara the false knight, and I should say what thou hast said, I should utter a most foul falsehood. To be the lady of the craven heart thou hast named, would be to become more wretched than now," answered Donna Maria, with spirit.

"Why wilt thou drive me to extremities with thy scorn? I will ask thee once more, and for the last time, wilt thou become my wife?"

Lara spoke in a deep and meaning tone.

"And once more and for the last time, I will not be thy wife. And now I will ask thee a question, and see that thou answer it, for it may be for the last time—wilt thou take me hence, and to my father's castle?"

"And I answer thee again, and for the last time, I will not, save as my lady."

"Then I shall never leave this fearful place. Thou hast my answer, why then shouldst thou persist?"

"Hear me, Donna Maria, and mark me well; thou shalt be mine—by fair or foul means, as thou wilt. I have spoken thee fairly, but thou hast forced me to be cruel."

"Thou speakest falsely. I have entreated thee to be merciful."

"Then first show mercy to me."

"Thou profanest the term in the sense thou dost use it. Thou dost not ask mercy, but love, and I cannot give it thee. Be content."

"Since thou canst give me no hope, however cold and remote, of winning thee by words poured forth on bended knee and from a true heart; since thou canst not extend to me the love thou hast in other years lavished upon another ; since thou hast steeled thyself against me ; since there is no chord of mercy in thy bosom ; since my presence fills thee with loath-ing ; since all else hath failed; since thou art beyond the reach of those who would gladly aid thee in this thy hour of need; since thou art here and among my creatures ; since thou art wholly in my power ; since thou art alone with me ; since thy cries will arise unheeded or un-heard ; since thy beauty hath inflamed my bosom and deprived me of reason; since thy disdainful words and high-born scorn hath left me no other alternative—I will do that which is unlike Lara—but I swear thou shalt not be dishonoured without remedy—thou shalt after this be the lady of Lara. Peerless Maria! thou shalt be mine, though thou and my God should never forgive me."

With eyes that burned like coals in their sockets, with features swollen with passion, with heaving breast, with arms outstretched with a look of inexpressible desire, Lara sprang forward.

" Hold," cried Donna Maria, in a firm voice, "hold ! "   And she drew herself to a queenly height, and a dagger gleamed in her hand, and her eyes flashed fire.   " Hold, I bid thee in God's name !   Lay thy hand upon me, and as thou livest, and as heaven is above us, I will bury this dagger in my bosom."

The knight paused as though a thunderbolt had fallen at his feet.   Donna Maria had thrown aside her scarf, and the sharp dagger point was levelled at her heaving bosom.   Lara was irresolute.

" Another step, another inch, and I strike."

There was something too earnest and deep in the tones of the maiden to leave any doubt in relation to her purpose.   The knight was thwarted ; and there he stood, with foot thrown forward and arms outstretched ; but the blood flowed back from his cheek, and the fire of expectation that flashed from his eyes changed to astonishment and chagrin.   Without a word he bowed, turned on his heel, and left her mistress of the field.

The day passed on.   Maria had not rested for many hours, and excitement and fatigue rendered it needful.   She ventured to lie down upon a mattress, after being assured by the beldam that she should not be disturbed.   She found a temporary forgetfulness of her situation in a troubled sleep.

When she awoke the sun had passed the meridian.   She arose, thankful that she had thus far escaped the violence of Lara. "Trusty steel," she said, putting her hand to her bosom to draw forth the dagger that had availed her in that needful hour. It was not there. The beldam had taken it thence while she slept. This discovery filled her with alarm, and renewed all her apprehensions. She sat down and wept. She was somewhat calmer when told that Lara had gone, and would not return until the morrow.

That night when her broken dreams came, there came also a vision of the gallant youth who had knelt at her feet, long, long ago, on a bright summer day, when the birds sang and the sun shone; and she threw her arms out, and moaning in her restless slumbers, sighed forth his name. Then came that incomprehensible something which she could not understand —that strange sympathy which bound her to the Knight of Calatrava.

"This night will the noble Lara visit his captive bird," said the beldam, the next day.

"Then may I die ere the night," Maria replied.

The dreaded night came, and with it came an intense agony. Though it was spent in a state of fearful suspense, Lara came not. The morning dawned. Maria sang the song she had loved to sing in other days, and in which she had taken a melancholy pleasure.

The strain died away in pensive echoes. A step was heard without. The sound of voices was borne to her ears—a key turned in the door. The maiden held her breath in fear— the blood fled her cheeks. The door creaked on its hinges, opened, and Maria averted her gaze that she might not behold her persecutor.

"Maria!"

The tones were not those of Lara.

"Maria!"

That voice—holy virgin! it was like that which had come oft to her in dreams.

"Maria!"

The maiden turned to the speaker; the Knight of Calatrava stood before her. She trembled in every limb. That voice vibrated strangely upon the strings of memory.

"Thou hast sung a song," said the knight in a deep, low voice.

The maiden was silent, but still that voice, ever that voice.

"The burden of thy song was—was a gallant knight."

The speaker faltered, and some strong emotion seemed to shake him from head to heel.

"Thou didst love the knight who was the burden of thy song?"

Donna Maria wept.

"Maria!"

Mother of God! it was his voice. The knight threw up his visor.

"MARIA!"

A wild cry of joy escaped the lips of the maiden; she sprang forward and fainted in his arms. In the Knight of Calatrava she recognized the youth who had knelt at her feet on a bright summer day, long, long ago, when the birds sang and the sun shone.

He strained her to his heart in a dear em

brace ; he gazed into her eyes ; he called her by name a thousand, thousand times ; he warmed her back to life by his kisses. But that was no time for the sweet dream of love. He was encompassed by dangers—he must bear her to a place of safety.

"Lead me to the court by the shortest way," he said to the knave at the door.

His order was obeyed, and in his arms he bore his half unconscious burden to the air. Two steeds, housed and barded, were waiting him there. The fresh air revived Maria. He placed her upon one of the horses—he mounted the other, and giving the letter and the ring to his faithful squire, with his dear love he galloped away.

CHAPTER XIII.

A JOURNEY.—A MEETING.—FOREBODINGS.

WHEN the maiden from over sea, and from regions of sultry suns, had swallowed a composing draught the Bohemian woman had prepared for her, she sank into a slumber, while her strange protectress sat by her lowly couch. She awoke refreshed.

"Now shalt thou go to thy mistress, thou daughter of Palestine," said the woman.

Saracena arose quickly to her feet and wrapped her mantle about her slender person.

"I am ready," she said, and followed the uncanny woman from the hut. At a short distance therefrom two horses were fastened to a tree. Saracena questioned not who brought them or whence they came. She was assisted into the saddle by the woman, who, mounting the other horse, bade her follow. How strange was the contrast between the pair as they rode on—the one was withered and old, the other beautiful and young. 'Tis often thus in life opposites are brought together, and often in some incomprehensible way our destinies are linked with the lowest.

Great as was the difference—as badly as they were mated—Saracena feared her not. Since their first conversation her fears had vanished, and she confided herself to her care without a doubt of her good faith. They took the direction towards the valley where dwelt the wandering people, and the journey thither was long and painful to Saracena, who was un-used to hardship. By the same winding sub-terraneous way that we are already acquainted with, she was conducted to the presence of her mistress. Joyful was the meeting between them, though their separation had been but for a day—but a day of suffering and painful sus-pense. Donna Teressa had of course been borne directly to the cavern which they reached by daylight, by dint of rapid travelling. No in-sult was offered her on the way. The orders of Sir Haro and the Bohemian leader were strictly obeyed, and, as may well be imagined, the ride was one of extreme terror, and replete with anxious forebodings. By keeping the appoint-ment with Sir Haro, she had learned nothing of her lover, and what was worse, thrown her-self into the power of a false knight, from whom she had all to fear that fair lady can. She was now far from those who loved her—

far from those whose strong arms would gladly
protect her.   She had hazarded all, and had
lost.   Fortune was not propitious.   She must
now bow to her destiny, however dark it might
be.   Here, shut up in the earth, buried alive,
with no one to hear her cries, she would fall
an easy victim to him of the Steel Cross.

Although her heart bounded with joy at be-
holding the faithful Saracena, her transports
soon gave way to feelings less pleasing.   She
saw in this pure young creature only another
victim—another sacrifice to the wickedness of
Sir Haro.   She said:

"My girl, thou hast done wrong in coming
hither."

"Nay, dear lady, can I not suffer what thou
dost?" she said, fervently.

"No, no, thou canst not.   It may be that
which one had far better suffer than two—that
which may be worse—worse than death," replied the lady, wildly.

The features of the Saracen girl grew redder
than crimson—her eyes flashed like fire—her
slender figure trembled with indignation—the
deep high pride of her character and her sex
shone forth in a blaze.   She laid her tiny white
hand upon the beautifully jewelled dagger that
she always wore in her girdle, and at that moment she was a thing to look upon—a dear
divinity to worship.   Donna Teressa gazed upon her with inexpressible admiration, and O how
she loved her with her eyes! how she loved her
then!

"Let him dare," she cried, "let him dare so
much as look upon thee with an evil eye—let

him dare so much as lay his smallest finger upon thee!" And the dear girl made a gesture with her hand, that had a deeper meaning than all human words. "Ay, let him dare!"

Teressa sprang forward and folded the noble spirited creature to her heart.

"How much I love thee! With one like thee I must indeed be safe. To one so pure, so generous, so lovely, so devoted, the least insult can never be offered," said the lady, earnestly.

"In the very extremity of our need, when there is no other hope—when the worst stares us in the face, and ruin shrieks in our very ears, there will be to the poor Saracen girl a pleasure in dying with her mistress," replied Saracena.

"Amen! let it be so—let this be the compact between us. And now let us beguile the weary hours as best we may, and strive to forget that which may come. Sing unto me, Saracena, some of the pensive lays I have loved to hear in hours of gladness—when I was not held in durance, like a captive bird."

"What shall I sing, since it is thy pleasure?"

"What thou wilt. There is nothing which thou canst sing that will not be music to me, for to me thy voice is music ever."

"Then I will sing thee one which a certain youth, which I will not tell thee of, sung beneath a window once on a time. I had been singing the songs of my native land, which thou knowest of. When I had ceased, I heard the song which I will sing thee, and I knew the tones that sang it well. I will not tell thee whither it pleased me."

"Ah, thou needest not, Saracena. I doubt not it was the handsome page who came with the Moorish knight from Toledo, who sang beneath thy window, once on a time."

"Thou shalt think as thou wilt. But list thou to the song:

SONG.

"In the bright hour of morning,
  The dark night of rest,
My wild thoughts shall wander
  To her I love best.
I will not forget thee,
  Thou daughter of my song,
And the heart in my bosom
  Shall sigh for thee long.

"They'll ever be near thee,
  Those stray thoughts of mine,
And whisper their meaning,
  Dear spirit, to thine.
The low words thus spoken,
  When woven in song,
Are, maiden, dear maiden,
  I'll sigh for thee long.

"A face gently beaming—
  A meek loving eye,
With intellect gleaming,
  Shall ever be nigh.
As I gaze on that vision,
  I'll sing that wild song—
Dear maiden! dear maiden!
  I'll sigh for thee long.

" As pure in its breathings
  As zephyr can be,
Is the love that I offer,
  Dear maiden, to thee.
Scorn it not, spurn it not,
  Then, idly away,
For a heart-love like mine,
  Is not won in a day.

" A spirit that's hopeful,
  A heart that is thine.
Is all that I lay
  At thy beautiful shrine.
I bring thee no riches,
  No wealth from the sea,
But the heart in my bosom
  Sighs ever for thee."

" A love-lorn ditty, truly, yet the measure
runneth smoothly," said Teressa, sadly. "Thy
memory is retentive."

" Maidens are not apt to forget such matters. Thine own memory can, it may be, bear
witness to this Hast thou not sung the song
of the Black Knight more than once? And
now wilt thou sing it to me?"

After a short pause the lady sang as follows:

" My heart is very sad this night—
  It ne'er shall blither be,
And though to-morrow's sun be bright,
  'Twill bring no joy to me.

" The thoughts that cheered me once have
      fled;
  O who would longer live,
When every pulse of joy is dead
  Life's changeful dream can give?

"The bird that mateless sings to-night,
　　With sad and wailing cry,
　May thrill its song at morning light
　　With blither heart than I.

"The mateless bird is free as air,
　　While I in durance pine ;
　It sings its wild song everywhere—
　　I would that I could mine.

"I know not what my lot may be,
　　What fate the dawn may bring—
　Perchance its light may shine on me,
　　A vile dishonoured thing."

There was a momentary silence when the song
ceased.　The maidens were startled by a slight
sound.　They raised their eyes, and Sir Haro
stood before them.　With a cry of fear the
maidens drew back, and nestled closer to each
other.　The Knight of the Steel Cross bowed
formally, saying, in a voice intended to be
agreeable :

"I have presumed to intrude myself upon
you for a few moments."

"Thou hast said well.　It is a piece of pre-
sumption that none but thou would be guilty
of—an intrusion we cannot forgive," retorted
Teressa, with haughty coldness.

"Lady, thy speech hath much of bitterness,"
replied Sir Haro, biting his lips.

"Hast thou the effrontery to speak of bitterness of speech, after the insult thou hast offered
me?　Away, thou of the craven heart, or make
the only atonement in thy power for this violence—take me to my father's castle."

"That I will not, for I cannot live without thee. I mean thee no harm; but on the contrary, I intended thee an honour. Thou shalt become my wife."

"Thy wife! I would sooner be thy slave," replied Teressa, indignantly.

'My slave!" responded Sir Haro, angrily.

"Ay, thy slave."

"Who am I?" he asked, proudly drawing himself up.

"Who art thou? I will tell thee, and see thou forget it not. Thou art a traitor, and a false knight—a disgrace to chivalry. Thou hast not earned the spurs upon thy heel."

"Traitor, sayest thou?" replied Sir Haro, turning pale. "What meanest thou? How darest thou throw scorn in my teeth?"

"How darest thou be a traitor? And how darest thou bring me hither? My heart can never tell thee half its scorn—my lips can never express to thee how truly I detest thee."

The bosom of Sir Haro swelled with rage. He bit his nether lip till the blood came. Advancing one foot, and stretching out one hand in a menacing manner, he said, in a hoarse voice:

"Lady, thy stinging words have sealed thy doom. Thou shalt never be the wife of Sir Haro."

"Thank God!" said both the maidens, in concert.

"Thank the demons as fittingly, for it is not in mercy I have said thou shalt not be the wife of Sir Haro. Knowest thou not thou mayest be something worse?"

"I know that I can be nothing half so vile as the wife of Sir Haro. There is not a thing that lives that I should not rather be."

"Have then thy choice. Thou shalt be—be—" And he whispered a word which made the maidens start.

"That is not half so bad," cried Teressa, scornfully. "Far better than thy wife. But that I shall never be. Do thy worst. I defy thee."

"What !"

"Hark ! let me breathe a word in thy ear — undo what thou hast done."

There was deep meaning in the words of the maiden.

"Nay, that I cannot, for THE HOUR has passed."

"Then another hour will soon come. Be warned—prepare."

"What wouldst thou say ? Thy words sound strangely," said Sir Haro, pressing his hand upon his brow.

"I say, Sir Haro, that there is ruin for thee —a ruin at thy very door. The bolt hangs over thy head by a single hair—it will fall on thee soon, and the house of Haro shall be no more."

As the excited maiden spoke, she drew up her beautiful figure, and some seemed she like a thing to bow down to. The knight recoiled, and put out his hands as though bidding her to stop.

"Sir Haro, know for a truth, that whatever unwarrantable power thou mayest exercise over me and my fortunes, that it will only be for a brief period. Do not turn away, for I would not that thou shouldst not hear the next words I am about to utter for a world. I shall live to witness thy doom."

The maiden looked a prophetess, as she stood then. The knight seemed bewildered. For a moment he had no power of words. When he spoke, he articulated with difficulty:

"Think not to intimidate me, or escape me so easily. This well-gotten-up scene shall avail thee nought. It shall rather hasten thy fall. That fair girl there, who clings to thee like thy other self, and whom thou lovest so dearly, shall be torn from thee this hour. Thou shalt never see her again."

"Nay, thou canst not do this—thou canst not be so cruel."

"I cannot be so cruel! Thou shalt see if I cannot. Come with me, my pretty one."

The knight of the Steel Cross stepped forward to lay his hands on Saracena.

"Beware!" said Saracena. "beware!" And again the tiny hand was laid upon the jewelled dagger hilt. "I will never leave her —thou canst not tear me from her with life. By the mother of God! if thou layest thy hand on me, I will strike thee with this dagger!"

The knight laughed in derision and made another step. It well nigh proved his last. A blow from a battle-axe laid him low.

A cry of joy burst from the lips of the maidens. The Black Knight and the handsome page were before them. What pen may tell the joy that gushes up from the very heart on the occasion of such a meeting? Not mine, *not mine.* Let others write when true lovers meet in the darkest hour. The Moorish knight drew his own Teressa to his bosom, and for other souls a mine of gold would not purchase the happiness he tasted then. During the time the page was busy with Saracena, and what he thought and what he said then, I cannot tell; but his tongue seemed eloquent, and his eyes beamed with pleasure.

" Wilt thou go with me ? " asked the Moorish knight of Teressa. And he spoke in a very low voice, and gazed into her eyes.

" I will go with thee," she replied, in the same tone.

"Then let us hence. We have no time to lose."

Taking the arm of the knight, they hastened from the cavern. They were followed by the page and Saracena. Sir Haro was left upon the earth where he had fallen.

At the mouth of the cavern were four gallant steeds, housed and barded, and fresh from stall. The parties were soon in the saddle and moving forward at a rapid rate. At a short distance from the valley the knight halted and blew a blast upon a bugle which hung at his girdle. From the group of trees near them sprang a score of Moorish knights in bright armour, such as would grace a king's court. They bowed in gallant style to the ladies, and then, at a signal from the Black Knight, they put spurs to their steeds and galloped away in a body towards Toledo. It was now deep night. For a brief space their course was marked by a stream of fire, and then the darkness shut down upon their track.

CHAPTER XIV.

THE DENOUEMENT.

WE will now look after our other characters. The Knight of Calatrava reached the castle of Guzman without accident. Don Lopez received him coldly. "I have the pleasure of restoring thy daughter, noble Guzman," he said.

"Those who hide can find ; and it is an old saying," replied Lopez, with a frown. Then turning, he embraced his daughter with right good-will, at the same time adding :

"Thou art now protected by the arm of thy father, my child. Scruple not to tell me all, as no promises extorted from thee by threats, and while thou wert in bodily fear, are binding. Speak, my daughter, unmask the villain."

At that moment Lara entered the hall. His quick conception took in all at a glance. His ruddy visage grew pale as marble. He grasped a chair for support. A wild surprise shot from his eyes.

"Ay, step forward, and congratulate thy friend on the recovery of his child !" repeated the Knight of Calatrava, ironically.

"Welcome, noble Lara, to my father's hall!" cried Donna Maria, advancing a step with much courtesy. "Thy former services render thy presence peculiarly agreeable and opportune! Why linger thy footsteps? Hast thou no word of greeting for the daughter of Guzman? "

Guzman gazed first at one and then at the other in mute astonishment.

"How ! what means this ?" he cried.

Donna Maria laid her hand on her father's

arm and held up the other towards Lara, who stood like one transfixed.

"Look! behold him who hath done this wrong—the abductor of thy daughter.   Looks he not like a craven heart, and a false knight?"

The features of the noble grew black with rage. "Begone!" he cried, in a voice of thunder; "begone, dissembling villain! begone, ere I order my menials to lay hands on thee—begone! and enter never again the halls of Guzman—away! ere I have thee scourged.   What! ho! ye menials— seize him, and take from him his spurs."

The menial throng rushed forward to put their master's orders in execution, but Lara turning, sprang away like lightning, covered with shame, and burning with mortification.

Guzman turned to the Knight of Calatrava, and putting his daughter's hand in his, said:

"Whoever thou art, brave knight, I have wronged thee much, and whoever thou art, my daughter is thine.   Thou shalt wed her to-morrow."

The knight bowed low, and replied without raising his visor, which he had kept closed from the first.

"I thank thee, noble and generous Guzman, for the priceless gift. It shall be mine to deserve the precious trust thou art this day reposing in me. Believe me, the house of Guzman will never be dishonoured by the Knight of Calatrava.   According to thy word, if it please the lady, let our nuptials take place ere this hour to-morrow."

"Well mayest thou believe the lady has no objections," replied Guzman, with a smile. "I read no unwillingness in her manner—no loathing in her eye."

"I have much to say to thee," said the Knight of the Iron Crest, "when a fitting opportunity offers."

"At thy own pleasure, sir knight; but at present rest is needful. When you both have refreshed yourselves with food and sleep, I will hear you."

A servant was about to conduct Alfonso to a chamber, when a page in rich attire entered the hall.

"I would see the Knight of Calatrava," he said, bowing low.

"I am he. What wouldst thou?" replied Alfonso.

The page approached. Bending his knee to the floor, he drew a ring from his bosom, and presented it to the Knight of Calatrava, saying:

"My master sent thee this ring." Alfonso started back as though a viper had stung him. There was a momentary silence. Recovering himself, the knight took the ring and placed it on his finger, saying:

"My word is sacred."

And then to Guzman—"Matters of the first importance—matters which will admit of no delay, force me to tear myself from your society for a time. I know not how long. Suffice it that my honour and my word would suffer by a moment's delay." He took the hand of Maria: "Doubt me not—fear not—question not, and if aught should happen to prevent my return, attribute it to my wayward destiny, and not to me. Farewell, my life—farewell, noble Guzman."

Bowing, the Knight of Calatrava followed the page. Mounting a horse from stall, he rode away with the page without question.

The feelings of Alfonso we will not attempt to portray. In a moment the cup of happiness was dashed from his lips—his union with Maria deferred for an indefinite period—perhaps for ever. Heavy was his heart when after a tedious journey he saw the wall of Toledo rising before him. To crown the unhappiness of Alfonso, he learned from a peasant what he knew not before, viz., that his sister had been decoyed into meeting with a knight, since which time nothing had been heard of her. This, as may well be imagined, alarmed him beyond measure. He would gladly have hastened to the paternal castle, to learn how far this report was true, and take some step for her recovery. But his promise to the unknown knight with whom he had jousted, and by whom he had been overthrown, prevented any movement in the matter at present.

Many questions arose in his mind to perplex him. Who was the unknown knight with whom he had jousted? What were his intentions? Many a worshipper of the prophet gazed in wonder at the Christian knight, who rode through the streets of Toledo, nor was their astonishment lessened when they saw him at the gate of the royal palace—the residence of Ali Maimon, the descendant of the great Abdalrahman. A forest of lances waved in grateful courtesy, as he passed through the court of the royal residence.

"This, then," said Alfonso, as he entered

the palace, "is the dwelling of the magnificent king—the generous monarch. How the world was cheated when Ali Maimon was born a follower of Mahomet. Here in this sumptuous palace hath been born a line of infidel kings, but none like him who now fills the throne— none so brave, none so noble, none so magnanimous. O thou follower of the Crescent, when wilt thou be a follower of the Cross? When wilt thou ride forth to do battle for the King of kings?"

The Knight of Calatrava passed on, dazzled on every hand by the glory of the Moorish sovereign. Wealth and splendour met his vision at every step. "This might well bring shame upon the court of Ferdinand. In Ali Maimon, the Infidel king, the Christian Ferdinand hath a noble enemy."

"Tarry thou here, noble knight," said the page.

The knight was left alone in a sumptuous apartment. He busied himself by examining the paintings that graced the walls. While thus engaged, he did not hear the footsteps of the belted knight, who entered unannounced. For a moment the knight regarded the noble figure of Alfonso with evident admiration.

Scorning to remain longer unseen, he struck his sword-hilt, as by accident upon his cuirass. It sent forth a sharp, ringing sound.

The Knight of Calatrava started, and laid his hand upon his blade. There was no cause for alarm. The Knight of the Crescent was before him. He stepped forward and greeted Alfonso with the kindness and courtesy of an old friend.

"I forget that I am not a guest, when the

Knight of the Crescent speaks," said Alfonso, with a smile, pointing to the ring upon his finger.

"And so I would have thee, thou of Calatrava. Thou art from this moment my guest."

"The Knight of the Crescent is still the same—still generous—not to be outdone in courtesy. I can scarce regret my journey to Toledo. But for one circumstance, I could wish myself in no other place."

The Moorish knight bowed low, and smiled significantly, saying:

"Thou wilt conquer me again, thou of the haughty crest."

Then, after a pause:

"Hast thou seen the Moorish monarch?"

"I have seen the noble Ali Maimon in mid-battle fighting like a lion, but never upon his throne like a king. I would fain see him thus."

"And thou shalt be gratified. To thy name and thy fame he is no stranger, and he hath oft spoken of Alfonso, the brother of Ferdinand, the king of Castile and Leon. I will first announce thee to the king, and thou shalt come after."

The Knight of Calatrava was again alone. A few moments only had elapsed, when the page again made his appearance, saying:

"Thou wilt follow me to the presence of Ali Maimon."

A few paces took them to the audience-chamber of the monarch. He was seated on a gorgeous throne, surrounded by all the insignia of royalty. Upon either hand was a wall of shields, and a forest of spears. Two stalwart knights with battle-axes stood near the throne, and still nearer as many pages attentive to the wants of their royal master. The king arose, and motioned Alfonso to approach. A cry of wonder passed his lips. He recoiled as if he had received a blow with a battle-axe. The Knight of the Crescent was upon the throne of Toledo—and his gallant foeman was the Moorish monarch.

"Approach, my gallant foeman, and brother of the Christian king," said Ali Maimon; and he stepped down from the throne, and took the knight by the hand.

"Nobly hast thou redeemed thy word. Thou hast followed my ring from the altar, and from lady's bower, and much shall it avail thee. Read this."

The king handed Alfonso a paper. He grew pale as he read it, and gasped for breath. It was a proclamation of Ferdinand, his brother, denouncing him as a traitor, and offering a reward for his head. Alfonso was astonished. He looked up at the Moorish monarch for the explanation his tongue refused to ask.

"It is the work of Sir Haro," said Ali Maimon, "and thine would have been a bloody bridal, hadst thou tarried but an hour at the castle of Guzman. The serpent hath filled the ears of thy sovereign, and thy brother, for thou art no traitor, or I no king."

Alfonso turned away his head, and his heart was heavy. The word "traitor" grated harshly upon his ear.

"Ah! it grieves thee to be branded a traitor.

but let it pass.   I swear by the tomb of the
prophet, that this stain shall be wiped away,
and the real traitor shall suffer."

"I thank thee, generous king.   Thou wert'
noble as an unknown knight, and thou art noble
as a monarch.   I would to God thou wert a
Christian," cried Alfonso, warmly.

"Thou wilt conquer me again," replied Ali
Maimon, with earnestness.   "But though thou
bowest to the Christ, and I to the prophet, it
hinders us not from being friends.   Thou shalt
be my guest until the king hath seen his error.
I make terms for thee not as a king, but according to our compact when I was an unknown
knight."

"All thou dost thou doest like a king," answered Alfonso.

"Flattery is the bane of monarchs, and yet
I love to hear the Knight of Calatrava," rejoined
the king.

"Didst thou not say to me, that but for one
circumstance thou couldst wish thyself in no
other place?"

"I did, king of Toledo."

"Name it, thou of Calatrava."

"As I journeyed hither, I met a peasant.
He told me that Donna Teressa, my sister, had
suddenly and mysteriously disappeared.   It
was rumoured that she had been abducted by a
Moorish knight, known as the Black Knight."

"Thou hast heard this but recently?"

"But recently, king."

"Knowest thou aught of this caballero
called the Black Knight, thou of the towering
crest?"

"I know nought of him save that he is not of my creed—that he is an accomplished knight, and that he hath appeared at sundry places when least expected."

"Hast seen him ever?"

"I have seen him in the listed plain only. Gallantly he sat his horse, and nobly he did his devoir, and though he be an enemy to my faith, he is nevertheless the flower of chivalry."

"Did this knight presume to love the sister of thy king?" asked Ali Maimon.

"So I have reason to believe," replied Alfonso.

"Did the fair lady, thy sister, love the presumptuous Black Knight?" continued the king of Toledo, earnestly.

"So it was rumoured, and I fear with too much truth," replied the Knight of Calatrava, seriously.

"I will put this Black Knight face to face with thee, and if he hath done this deed, it shall be thine to name his doom."

The king of Toledo receded a pace, and throwing off his polished steel plate, he stood before the wondering Alfonso, the BLACK KNIGHT, in simple haubergeon and hood of mail. Alfonso was dumb with amazement.

"Thinkest thou the Black Knight has done the deed thou hast named?" asked Ali Maimon, with a smile.

"I will strike him dead at my feet who dare affirm it!" cried Alfonso, with warmth, laying his hand on his sword.

"'Tis well. Thou art still the same, and the soul of chivalry."

The king turned, and made a signal to the knights who formed a solid phalanx near the throne. They opened to the right and left, and in the centre stood Donna Teressa.

Again the Knight of Calatrava was speechless with astonishment. By what agency was she there? What was to be the end of all this mystery?

Donna Teressa came forward, and embraced her brother, saying, gayly:

" Let nothing perplex thee, for this Moorish king is a magician."

" So it would seem," replied Alfonso, dubiously. "But, sister, how camest thou hither?"

" I came in goodly company—with the king of Toledo, and a score of dashing knights."

" Camest thou willingly?"

" Ay, with right good will."

"Thou speakest darkly. Explain, lest my thoughts do thee wrong."

Ali Maimon interposed. "It has been Ali Maimon's good fortune to wrest the most beautiful of women from the power of a villain. Sir Haro decoyed her from thy castle under the pretence of making certain important communications, and basely, by means of his creatures,. bore her away to the valley which thou knowest of. The wandering Bohemian, whom thou hast reason to remember, is the leader of the lawless men who dwell there, and was in my service. To me he hath proved faithful, and by my orders he hath been faithful to thee, or thou wouldst ere this have been in the power of Sir Haro. I went to Castile to woo thy sister, whom a strange chance had once thrown in my way. I went thither as the Black Knight, and there I wandered in various disguises. The prophet hath given me the power of thwarting a false knight—of serving fair lady—of saving thy life, and of doing service to thy king. False to a false knight, the wandering Bohemian has proved true to true men. While in thy service, and mine, he was also in the service of Sir Haro —a villain whom every true man will despise. I see thou art filled with wonder and gratitude; but not to me, to the bright eyes of Donna Teressa dost thou owe all this."

"And the palmer?" added Alfonso, hesitatingly.

"And the palmer I will show thee as soon as I can wave my wand," rejoined the king, gayly. Throwing off his harness of mail quicker than I write it, the palmer, in his woollen gown, with his pilgrim staff and escallop-shell, stood before the Knight of Calatrava.

"This Moorish monarch is indeed a magician," said he, turning to Teressa. "It may be that he hath the gift of second sight also," he added.

"Thou shalt see, O thou of the order of Calatrava," responded Ali Maimon "Again I I wave my wand, and yet again I change." The long woollen garment, with its cross and shell fell from the shoulders of the king, and drawing the pilgrim cap from his head, long white hairs streamed from beneath it. The old man of second sight was before them.

"I have no words!" said Alfonso. "Thou hast outdone me in all things. Sister, come hither. Give me thy hand. Generous monarch, thy hand. As the only gift in my power, I give thee the sister of a king, and may God bless thee as I would bless thee were I God."

"Thou hast outdone me again in generosity," said the king, in a subdued voice, and leading Teressa to the throne, he seated her thereon, saying, "Henceforth thou shalt share our throne."

"But the Knight of Calatrava is not quite happy," continued the king; "is there nothing we can do for him?" and he made another signal to the forest of lances on his right. Again they opened to the right and left, and Don Lopez de Guzman, Donna Maria, Don Rodrigo, and Ximena stepped forward.

"Let me explain again, O thou of Calatrava. Thy journey hither hath purposely, and by my orders, been by a circuitous way, by reason of which a day longer was required to perform it. During this time, I acquainted the noble Guzman, and the peerless lady his daughter, together with the valiant squire, with what was going forward. I knew by my secret agents that an order was issued for the arrest of Guzman at the same time thou wert charged with treason. I warned him of this and bade him fly, thither with his daughter for safety. The day succeeding the rescue of Donna Maria, a man in palmer's weeds journeyed with the two pages. One of them was very comely to look upon, and his cheek and his hand were like the cheek and hand of lady bright."

The king looked at Ximena. "They questioned the palmer in right comely phrase of a certain knight whom they served, and they questioned not in vain. The palmer was weary, and he mounted with one of the pages, and journeyed to a certain castle."

" The brigands, good king—thou hast said nought of the brigands! " interrupted Ximena. "To the gallantry of the bearer of palms do I owe my life," and Ximena bent the knee to Ali Maimon.

" Arise, I command thee, and hear, thou enchantress ; am I obeyed?" said the king with a smile.

" As I said, the palmer, and the delicate page, reached a deserted castle at deep midnight. In the chamber there was a broken image of the virgin; he knew there was a secret to unwind. Thither he conducted the pages, and kindled a fire upon the long deserted hearthstone. Thou knowest that the castles of feudal lords were built in troublous times, and have secret ways and sliding panels which have been used for various purposes." Ali Maimon looked significantly at Alfonso and Rodrigo.

" The very words," said the former, in a low voice.

"The man of the pilgrim staff and escallop-shell, and the pages had not been long in the chamber where lieth the broken image of the virgin, when, by some strange magic, the wall suddenly opened, or seemed to open and out sprang a gallant youth in armour from head to heel, with sword in hand, and demanded an explanation of what he saw. The page with the woman's voice, and woman's hand, and woman's cheek, flew to his arms, whereupon the fiery youth dropped his weapon and— and—"

"Stop, I command thee, king as thou art!"

exclaimed Ximena, putting her hand playfully upon his mouth.

"Wilt allow this tyranny?" cried the king, turning to Teressa.

"Ay, truant monarch, I will allow it, and look well that thou hast not worse tyrant to command thee."

"The youth," resumed the king, "who sprang from the wall was not unlike this youth,' pointing to Rodrigo, "and the page with the woman's hand was not unlike this fair lady," looking at Ximena.

"And the palmer," added Ximena, "was not unlike this noble Moorish knight," pointing to the king.

"When greetings and mutual explanations had passed between the page and the youth," continued Ali Maimon, "the palmer warned the latter of the danger that menaced his valiant master and himself, and that the knight he served had already sought safety with the king of Toledo.

"'Fly thither at once,' said the pilgrim, 'and fail not to take this fair page with thee. At a short distance from the valley thou knowest, where the man of second sight met thee, thou wilt find a troop of Moorish lancers. Give them this,' and the palmer gave the youth a ring, 'and bid them escort thee to Ali Maimon.' Ye gallant knights and fair ladies, is not the riddle read?"

"It is read!" they responded with one voice; "and there is no king like Ali Maimon, the descendant of the great Abdalrahman."

"I perceive there is yet one thing wanting

o complete our mutual happiness. Let me
wave my wand again and for the last time."

Again there was an opening in the forest of
spears and the wall of shields. Forth stepped a
man of God, followed by the Bohemian and his
gaunt spouse—the wandering weird woman.

"Welcome, thou man of God! welcome, thou
son of Roma! and welcome, thou wandering woman of the fierce eye and the strange spirit!"
exclaimed the king. The welcome was reiter-
ated with right goodwill by the goodly company.

"Thou sullen and yet faithful son of a wandering people, and thou his spouse, henceforth
your home shall be in the walled cities, or in
the valleys, or upon the sunny mountains of
our dominions, as shall suit your mood. Ali
Maimon hath gold in his coffers; when you
need it, ask, for he hath never been branded a
niggard, and those who have served him he for-
gets not," said the Moorish monarch.

The wandering Bohemian advanced a step,
and stretched out his hand. His manners had
in nothing changed from the first. The same
waywardness of spirit, the same wild moodiness
gleamed from his eyes.

"I thank thee, O thou king of the Busnos,
for the words thou hast spoken; but the swart
son of Roma needs nothing. He will not tarry
within the walled city of the munificent king,
but he will wander in the fertile valleys, and
dwell upon the sunny mountains, as he has
been wont from childhood. The leopard cannot
change his spots, nor the Ethiopian his skin,
neither can he change his nature. If he hath
served ye he is glad.

The Bohemian bared his dark bosom, and displayed a frightful wound thereupon.

"Heed it not, thou upon the throne, heed it not, and let it not cause thee, or thine, one pulse of joy the less. The dark son of Bohemia will away to the hills of the Moorish monarch, to the cliffs of the valleys, and the caves of the earth."

The Bohemian receded from the throne, and ere the king had time to reply, the gaunt woman stepped forward. Her tall bony figure was drawn to its highest proportions. She stretched out her tawny hand. Her eyes flashed with a wilder fire than ever before.

"Listen, O thou upon the throne! Listen to the woman of the strange spirit. For the last time I will speak to thee, for the stars and the moon admonish me that my hour is near. Thy future shall be more glorious than thy past. Thy reign shall be most happy of all the kings of the land. Be kind to the dark children of my people, let thy hand be over them in mercy, let their home be for ever in thy realm, and undisturbed." The wandering woman paused, and motioned Saracena to approach.

"Come hither, thou from over sea, and from the regions of sultry suns," she said, in a commanding voice The Saracen maiden obeyed.

"Look thou upon this maiden—look upon her well, for she is thy brother's child. In the wars in Palestine thy brother Abdallah fought and fell; out ere then, he had loved the mother of this young creature. The wandering woman was there. She saw the knight dying upon the battle-field, and he charged her, and he gave her gold to bring his love-child to Toledo, and

lay it at thy feet. She bore it in safety to Castile, and gave it to the lady who will be thy
queen.   The dying knight, thy brother, gave
me these baubles, and I have kept them for the
love-child of the Moor."

The woman drew a casket from her bosom,
and gave it to Ali Maimon. "And now I go out
from before thy face, O thou king of Toledo, to
return no more. I go to fulfil my days in the
pleasant land."

Saracena was kneeling at the feet of the king.
The weird woman caught her in her brawny
arms, and for a brief moment strained her to
her wrinkled bosom. "Bless thee, bless thee!
thou from over sea, and may the way of thy
feet be thornless and smooth. My work in the
walled city is done."

The wandering woman drew her coarse garments about her, and strode rapidly away after
the Bohemian.

" Stay, good woman, stay !" cried the king.
His words fell on heedless ears. The woman
had gone.

Ali Maimon and Teressa eagerly examined
the casket. It contained jewels of immense
value, with a note traced by the hand of the
dying warrior. It read:

"My king, and my brother, be a father to
my love-child, and the blessing of Allah, and
the smiles of the prophet, reward thee. My
eyes grow dim, and the giddiness of death is in
my brain. I can write no more. The wandering woman who brings thee this, will tell thee
all. I die—I die—farewell."

And now the man of God did his work. Marriage contracts were drawn up and signed. Teressa was made in reality a queen, and, what was far better, the wife of Ali Maimon. The knight of Calatrava was wedded to Donna Maria. Don Rodrigo was knighted by the king, after which he was wedded to Ximena. Saracena, was betrothed to the handsome page who sung beneath her window once on a time. Thus all parties had their happiness consummated, and such bridals were never before in Toledo.

The day after the festivities were at an end, news was brought to Toledo of the death of Ferdinand, and that 'Don Alfonso, his brother, was to be his successor to the throne. When the Knight of Calatrava left Toledo, he left it to reign over Castile and Leon. Nugnez de Lara joined the brigands who dwelt in the castle, and soon after fell in a fray with the Bohemians. Sir Haro was condemned and executed for treason before the death of Ferdinand.

Poor Mina wandered and sang for many months among the wilds, but finally became rational, and the evening of her days passed in comparative happiness. Leaving all parties happy and content, I bring my romance to a close, hoping in my heart that the reader has been amused by the foregoing delineations.

www.ingramcontent.com/pod-product-compliance
Lightning Source LLC
Chambersburg PA
CBHW030548040726

47497CB00008B/2620